She was a vision . . .

The woman was so beautiful she seemed to shimmer. Could it be his imagination, or the dim, romantic cast of the moonlight? It was as if she'd been dusted with tiny sparkles.

Rowan couldn't take his eyes off this fairy princess who'd just swept into the Firecracker Ball, completely without warning. She gazed at him from behind a cat-eyed mask, with eyes that were violet-blue.

"Who are you?" he asked, cursing the rough catch in his voice.

Wordlessly, she smiled. She held up half a bottle rocket.

His pulse speeded as he found his own rocket. He thanked God for the silly game the hosts had devised of pairing up couples with bottle rockets that fit together. He knew it would be a perfect union.

He noticed that her hand trembled as much as his as they slid the pieces together. It was a perfect fit.

"I think this means you're mine," he murmured, and he pulled her into his arms.

ABOUT THE AUTHOR

Julie Kistler is a lifelong resident of the Midwest, where the winters are so cold, even the heartiest Midwesterners stay indoors and find something romantic to do. One of the many activities is dreaming of summer, and that's one reason Julie set *Cinderella at the Firecracker Ball* smack-dab in the middle of a sultry Wisconsin July. Julie loves fireworks, masquerade balls, beauty pageants and fairy tales, and they all managed to find their way into the story. Julie and her husband live with their cat, Thisbe, in the small town of Mahomet, Illinois, where Julie splits her time between writing and daydreaming.

Books by Julie Kistler

HARLEQUIN AMERICAN ROMANCE

158—THE VAN RENN LEGACY
207—CHRISTMAS IN JULY
236—WILDFLOWER
266—ALWAYS A BRIDESMAID
329—BEST WISHES
418—CHRISTMAS IN TOYLAND
429—FLANNERY'S RAINBOW
471—FINN'S ANGEL
485—BLACK JACK BROGAN

Don't miss any of our special offers. Write to us at the following address for information on our newest releases.

Harlequin Reader Service
P.O. Box 1397, Buffalo, NY 14240
Canadian address: P.O. Box 603,
Fort Erie, Ont. L2A 5X3

JULIE KISTLER

CINDERELLA AT THE FIRECRACKER BALL

Harlequin Books

TORONTO • NEW YORK • LONDON
AMSTERDAM • PARIS • SYDNEY • HAMBURG
STOCKHOLM • ATHENS • TOKYO • MILAN
MADRID • WARSAW • BUDAPEST • AUCKLAND

To Anne Stuart, a wonderful and talented author. Not everyone can say she almost broke up the Beatles, or that "Something in the Way She Moves" was written just for her. You foxy devil!

ISBN 0-373-16511-0

CINDERELLA AT THE FIRECRACKER BALL

Copyright © 1993 by Julie Kistler.

Prologue

September, 1972

"Clemmy Bede's a bastard," taunted Karla Farley, crossing her eyes and sticking out her tongue. "And everybody in the whole school knows it!"

Her equally hideous twin sister, Darla, giggled and ran around to Clementine's other side, hemming her in. "Bastard, bastard!" she shouted gaily.

But Clementine stood her ground, balling her hands into little fists. "Shut up! You just shut up, you... you..." She pulled the most highfalutin words she could think of out of this week's spelling list. "You two are nothing but pustules on the posterior of a bovine. But you're too stupid to even know what that means!"

"You take that back, Clemmy Bede, or I'll tell my mama what you said." Karla's lips curled in an evil smile. "She says you're no good anyway, because you ain't got a daddy and you're a little bastard child."

"My father is handsome and strong and brave!" Clementine shouted. "Better 'n your ugly old father any day."

"Yeah, and what's his name?" Karla squinted her eyes. "*We* got a real father. Our daddy is the biggest man in this town. We got our own factory, Clemmy Bede, and you ain't got nothin'."

"Your mama never got married, Clemmy," Darla chimed in. She stuck a plump finger right in Clementine's face. "She never got married but she had you, anyway. Our mama told us your mama is a disgrace and so are you."

"I am not a disgrace," she whispered. She could feel tears welling up in her eyes, but she didn't cry. She wasn't going to cry in front of those damn Farley brats.

She felt better already, just thinking the word *damn*. It was a bad word, a word with power and strength, and she rolled it around in her mind. Damn Karla to hell, and damn Darla, too! She smiled, knowing how mad her mother would be if she read Clementine's mind and saw two such bad words, and both in the same sentence.

"Are too a bastard," Karla insisted, but the bell rang, overriding her fit of temper. When recess was over, even the Farley girls had to go back inside. Hand in grubby hand, they raced off, flinging back more words that were lost in the breeze.

Clementine waited a few extra seconds, watching her enemies bolt inside the door to Homer T. Sparks Elementary School. She didn't care if she was late. Everybody knew she was the smartest girl in the third grade, and Miss Pine wasn't going to fuss just because she meandered in a few minutes after the rest of her class.

"Clemmy, you don't want to be late" was all Miss Pine would say. She had better things to worry about, like Karla and Darla's tantrums, or Jimmy Gooch, who never had paper to write on because he was always making spit wads.

Clementine stayed where she was on the empty playground, mulling over the word *bastard* and how it related to her. She knew she had a father. She just didn't know who or where he was. She had asked her mother a few times, but Mama didn't say, just patted her on the head and looked as if she might cry. Clementine had learned not to ask, because she didn't want to make Mama so sad.

But in her heart, she knew her father was someone very special—someone who would be with her if he could. He just couldn't, because he was an astronaut, or a spy, or maybe even an enchanted prince.

"Someday my father will come home, and he'll make those Farley brats pay," she vowed. "And, and...someday I'm going to be smart and rich and pretty and I'm going to make Karla and Darla eat dirt."

She laughed, feeling much better now that she had a plan. "Pustules on the posterior of a bovine," she said out loud, as she skipped across the playground. "Yessir, that's what they are."

Chapter One

All in all, Clementine Jemima Bede was having a very good day. She'd just swung another lucrative deal to remodel an old barn into a vacation house for a couple of rich Chicagoans, and she'd gotten an embarrassingly hefty check and a thank-you note from a satisfied customer.

"We love our barn!" the woman had written. "All of our friends are jealous, and we'll certainly send them on to you if you want the business."

Did she want the business? C.J. smiled. Did she ever!

"Life is lovely," she said to no one in particular, since she was alone in the rehabbed milking shed she called the offices of Redux Deluxe. Adjusting her baseball cap, she leaned back in the antique dentist's chair she used as office furniture and reached for the morning paper.

All C.J. needed to make this day absolutely perfect was a look at the stock quotes. If the price of Farley Fireworks stock had dipped again, C.J. would dance and whoop and yell. A few more points, and Farley Fireworks would be too far down the dumper for ol'

Buzz to pull it out. She was counting on it. Business success was sweet, but revenge against the Farley family was like eating honey fresh out of the hive.

"Nothing better," she said with satisfaction, cranking the chair into more of a reclining position and pulling the Sparks *Sentinel* into her lap. But before she could open it to the business section, her eyes lit on the front page. She shot up in her seat, almost dropping the whole thing.

"'The Prince of Takeovers visits Sparks,'" she read aloud. "This can't be." But it was. She kept reading, and it kept getting worse. "Speculation continues that Rowan McKenna is interested in taking over the ailing Farley Fireworks factory."

There he was, big as life, photographed as he bought an ice-cream cone on Main Street in downtown Sparks. She'd have to take the *Sentinel*'s word for it that it was Rowan McKenna, since all you could see in their out-of-focus photo was one ear, a piece of his shirt and the ice-cream cone, but who else would it be? Everybody in town knew one another, and they also knew how to spot tourists from a mile away. If this guy didn't fit either category, Odell Watson, who ran the newspaper, would have sniffed him out in two seconds flat.

She went back to the story accompanying the grainy photo. "The corporate raider, known in financial circles as the Prince of Takeovers, managed his first leveraged buyout when he was only 21 years old. Does McKenna have his raider's eye on Farley Fireworks? Only time will tell. McKenna has never gone for such a small operation, but Farley Fireworks is ripe for the plucking."

Ripe for the plucking? Of course it was! C.J. slammed the paper down on her desk. Pounding Farley Fireworks into oblivion was the whole point, and the goal behind two long years of careful financial plotting and several tricky maneuvers that skirted the edge of legality. Now, just when C.J.'s plans were about to bear fruit, in danced the Prince of Takeovers, ready to nab *her* prize.

"Not if I have anything to say about it." C.J. scanned the lines again. Maybe it was all a mistake, or an exaggeration. Maybe the man was taking a vacation, like most everyone else who passed through the Sparks area in the summer. She could hope, couldn't she?

"'Does McKenna have his raider's eye on Farley Fireworks? Only time will tell,'" she read out loud.

But she needed to know now. Right now. She'd been waiting for so long—all these years—to get her revenge against Buzz Farley and his horrible family. There was no way on God's green earth she was going to stand by while some hotshot corporate raider who couldn't care less about Buzz, or his pathetic wife, Mim, or their odious daughters, Karla and Darla, swooped in and ruined everything.

C.J. set her jaw. She could still hear the voice of the child she had been, vowing vengeance against the man who had wronged her mother. Who is my father? had been the recurring question of her childhood. At first she was sure he was a hero, a prince. But when push came to shove, when all the sordid details were out, she knew her father was no prince. Her father was Buzz Farley. Just thinking about it, her mouth curled in disgust.

Buzz Farley, owner of the fireworks factory, leading citizen of Sparks, father to that detestable duo, Karla and Darla . . . And he was C.J.'s father.

If it weren't so pitiful, it might've been tragic.

C.J. held her head up with pride. Fortunately, she bore no traits of the Farley gene pool. She didn't look or act or even smell like the Farleys, thank goodness. Of course, her mother had a few demerits against her name, too, for sleeping with Buzz Farley in the first place. But Ivy Bede had always been sweet and kind and more than a little dim, so it was hardly her fault when she fell in love with a heel like Buzz. Especially since he was her boss. Mama swore ol' Buzz had been good-looking and very dynamic in the old days, not to mention as rich and powerful as it got in Sparks, Wisconsin, population 823.

C.J.'s mother had been his secretary when he first started to run the fireworks factory, and when she got pregnant, everyone in town knew who was responsible. Not that that made a particle of difference to Buzz Farley. He went ahead and married the simpering Mim, daughter of a wealthy manufacturer from Milwaukee, and out popped Karla and Darla some five months after the wedding, only two months after Ivy Bede gave birth to her daughter, Clementine.

"You should've moved far, far away, Mama," C.J. had said. But Ivy Bede had stuck it out, year after year, and C.J. was stuck in this damned town with her.

From the time she was old enough to understand the whispers and the gossip, C.J. had promised her mother and herself that she would get out of Sparks, and that someday she would come back. And when she came back, she swore she would make them all pay.

So now here she was, so many years later, so close to her goal that she could smell victory in the air. Until the Prince of Takeovers waltzed into town and threatened everything she'd worked for.

Could he really be planning to buy the factory? C.J. chewed on the end of a rough fingernail. Even if McKenna looted the firecracker factory the way he had the other companies he'd taken over, smashing Buzz Farley's pride to smithereens, it wouldn't be the same. What good was revenge when somebody else's hand was twisting the knife?

"No way," she muttered.

"No way what?"

She glanced up in surprise. While she'd been sitting there stewing over the newspaper story, someone had edged inside her door.

"Oh my..." was all she managed to say, as she looked him up and down.

"Rowan McKenna," he offered, extending a hand.

She stayed where she was, safely behind her desk, refusing to rise to the bait and actually touch him. "The Prince of Takeovers," she whispered. In the flesh. It was as if she'd conjured him up just by reading the article about him. She'd harbored a few hopes that it would all turn out to be a mistake, an illusion, and that the Prince of Takeovers would fade away and never come back. But this man was no illusion.

No, he was only too real. As he looked down at her, he smiled, flashing white teeth in a chiseled face, and she knew she was a goner. She'd met predators before, Buzz Farley among them. But she'd never seen a wolf like this one, in Prince Charming's clothes. Rowan McKenna was gorgeous, slick as a whistle, dressed to kill. He had dark hair, not quite black, wavy and thick, beautifully cut to just brush his collar and look like a million bucks.

His eyes were light, a crystal-clear blue, framed by spiky dark lashes. There was only one word for eyes like that. Devastating.

Out of the paper and into her office, like magic, with his damn blue eyes and his damn sexy smile. But why? Could he possibly know she was the one who'd primed Farley Fireworks for the kill? Her stomach did a quick polka at the notion she'd been found out, but she regained her composure quickly.

No, he couldn't possibly know. No one knew, and no one even suspected. Why would they? On the surface, C.J. was a successful architect and builder, with no connection to Buzz Farley's slow, painful decline.

So what in God's name was Rowan McKenna doing here?

"Can I help you with something?" she asked quickly.

Biting the bullet, she realized she couldn't cower behind her desk forever. She stood up, brushing dust off the front of her jeans, feeling a momentary pang of regret that she'd visited a rehab site this morning, meaning she was dressed like one of the guys. She was wearing her oldest pair of jeans, tucked into construction boots. Over that, she had a man's white undershirt and a flannel shirt, so worn out that the plaid had pretty much disappeared. The long, pale strands of her hair were twisted into a braid and folded up under a dirt-streaked baseball cap, with the brim tipped down over her eyes. She would've wagered there were probably smudges on her face, as well.

If it wasn't her most attractive look, it was certainly the most typical. Every person in Sparks would've recognized this getup as quintessential C.J.

"Why don't you ever dress nicely?" her mother despaired, on the rare occasions they got together. "Clemmy, honey, you could look downright pretty if you'd just wear a skirt every once in a while, and maybe a little makeup." But C.J. clung to her jeans and her baseball cap, secure in the knowledge that nobody gave her a second glance when she was dressed this way. She felt invisible, and she liked feeling that way just fine.

But right now, the Prince of Takeovers was looking her up and down, and she didn't feel invisible. Not at all. If she didn't get a grip, she'd blush under the intensity of that gaze. Luckily, he couldn't see much of her face, since the peak of her baseball cap kept it in shadow, and even if she blushed, he'd never know. Besides, his interest wasn't so surprising. Like most men who walked in her door, he was probably confused, wondering how she figured into the equation at Redux Deluxe. Too dirty to be the secretary, and too female to be the boss. She'd seen that speculative look before.

"I came to see C. J. Bede," he said, consulting a slip of paper in his hand. "Is he around?"

"There is no *he,*" she told him. "I'm C. J. Bede."

"You're the builder?"

"Yes," she returned. Hadn't she just told him that? She was rapidly becoming annoyed with the Prince, no matter how good he looked. And so she fired a salvo of her own. "Is there a reason you're here, Mr. McKenna, or did you just pop in to quiz me on my identity?"

"Touchy, aren't you?" His tone was amused, teasing, as he smiled again, dishing out all sorts of excess charm. "How do you do any business when you're such a prickly little thing?"

She couldn't have said which she resented more, the "prickly" or the "little thing." Well, she supposed she'd been called worse. Ignoring the insults, C.J. folded her arms over her chest and rested her bottom on the edge of her desk. "My business is booming, thank you."

"Is it?"

C.J. gave him a more intent look. "Is there a reason you want to know, Mr. McKenna?"

"Call me Rowan," he said pleasantly. But he didn't answer her question, just skirted around her and made a big deal out of scanning the things she'd put up on her walls. "Clementine?" He leaned in closer to one of her diplomas. "Clementine Jemima Bede. That's...different."

While he played detective, C.J. began to feel very agitated about his slow, studious scrutiny of her personal items. Why did he care what she put on her walls?

"Look, Mr. McKenna," she began, spinning around to face him, to get to the reason for his surprising appearance at her office once and for all. "I don't want to..."

But he was tracing the words of a cross-stitched sampler she'd made when she was in a high school home economics class, and her words died on her lips.

That sampler was very special to her, very private, and the way his finger lingered over her stitches made her very uncomfortable. Itching to throw herself in between him and the artwork in question, C.J. kept her place on the desk instead.

"'Heav'n has no rage, like love to hatred turn'd. Nor hell a fury, like a woman scorn'd,'" McKenna read aloud. "Odd thing to choose for your wall, Clementine. Woman scorned, huh?"

Her home ec teacher hadn't been thrilled when she'd chosen the quote for her cross-stitch assignment, but she saw no reason to share that with Rowan. "I prefer C.J. to Clementine, if you don't mind."

"But I do mind. Clementine," he said again, letting her name linger on his lips. "I like it."

"Well, I don't," she said tartly.

But all the Prince did was send his hot gaze licking up and down her body, the same way he had when he'd first come in. "You know, Clementine, you don't look like the 'woman scorned' type to me."

Was that a compliment or an insult? Warily she asked, "Why not?"

"You look like you wouldn't tolerate being scorned." A spark of humor lit the depths of those crystal blue eyes. "You'd just belt the guy and move on."

"Yeah, I probably would," she admitted. "But it's not about me, anyway. It's an, um, old family heirloom."

"Old family heirloom?"

She just knew he was about to bring up the matter of her initials and the date, so carefully worked into the corner of the sampler. Before he had a chance, she

took the offensive. "You didn't come here to discuss
my wall hangings. So let's put our cards on the table.
What the heck are you doing here?"

He paused. Finally he offered, "I'm thinking about
finding a refuge, a summer house, somewhere to
spend my leisure time."

Leaving her cross-stitch behind, he walked toward
the pictures of rehabbed barns she'd filled the opposite wall with. There were interiors and exteriors, big
ones, small ones, red ones, white ones and even one
lovely barn that was bright blue. But they all represented successful conversion projects; from unused old
outbuildings, they'd become very nice homes. Unfortunately she couldn't imagine Rowan McKenna in any
of them.

"And you're telling me you want one of my barns
to use as your retreat?" she asked dubiously. "I don't
think I believe you, Mr. McKenna."

"Everybody needs a vacation, Clementine." He
shrugged, sticking his hands in the pants pockets of his
sinfully expensive suit. "Even me."

But she still wasn't buying. Men like the Prince
didn't show up and move into barns, no matter how
charming. They bought condos overlooking chic golf
courses, or rented villas on glittering islands where
they could dock their yachts. C.J. wasn't fooled. The
simple pleasures of Sparks, Wisconsin, wouldn't keep
Rowan McKenna occupied for five minutes. "And
what made you choose little old Sparks for your vacation home?"

"I haven't chosen yet," he said evenly. "That's why
I'm here. To get some more information before I make
up my mind."

"What kind of information?"

"About the town, the area." Casually he said, "I'd like to get the inside scoop on the Sparks community, to see if I've chosen wisely, before I make any kind of investment here. Investment in a vacation home, that is."

She considered whether he was telling the truth. It was possible, all right, but not probable. No, there was still something fishy about the Prince's interest in the area, not to mention his interest in Clementine Jemima Bede. She would've bet a million bucks he had no intention of finding a summer retreat.

"And why exactly did you think I'd have the information you were looking for?" she asked carefully.

He smiled again. His smile was smooth and gorgeous, but her suspicions increased as she thought again how much he resembled a predator.

What nice teeth you have, Mr. McKenna.

The better to eat you with, my dear.

Instead, he told her, "As a builder, you have to assess the relative benefits of different locations all the time. That gives you the kind of critical eye I need. Your office is a good five miles west of town, which makes you a bit of an outsider, which I also like. Plus I hear you do business all over the area, wherever there's a barn that suits your purposes. That gives you a perspective the people in town don't have."

"Mmm." The picture he'd painted—of her as a wise businesswoman, a sage counselor—was flattering, but hardly relevant. "First off, I build where there's a barn that somebody wants. No 'critical eye' involved. Second, I was born and raised in Sparks, so I'm hardly an outsider."

"That's not the impression I got from some of the folks in town."

Aha! So he was basing his opinion on what the town gossips had told him. She could just hear them now. "That C.J. Bede is a strange one, a real character. Doesn't get along with the regular folks in town, and lives way out in the middle of nowhere, in an old barn that ain't fit for humans, with that old bird Miss Prudence Hopmiller the only neighbor for miles."

"Well," she said tersely, "if they told you you could drop in here and I'd badmouth Buzz and the gang, they steered you wrong."

"Buzz?"

"Buzz Farley," she supplied, as if he didn't know. "Everyone says you're thinking of taking over his fireworks factory, so I'll bet you're digging for dirt on him and the town, and you thought an 'outsider' like me would be happy to provide it."

"Would you?"

"No," she returned evenly. "I wouldn't."

But he made no move to leave. "Well," she said briskly, "I'd love to chat with you about Sparks and all its joys, but I'm very busy." She pushed past him, making a good show of stacking the loose papers tossed on her old wooden filing cabinet and then carrying them back to the desk. "Too busy to fill in for the Sparks Tourist Bureau at the moment. So why don't you mosey back into town and look up Vesta Smalls, the town real estate agent? Vesta is real friendly, especially to men over eighteen and under seventy, and I'm sure she'd be happy to give you your fill of all kinds of pertinent facts about Sparks."

He just stood there, looking at her, clearly unamused. C.J. got the idea that he wasn't any too hot on looking for Vesta. Pity. Vesta would've tried her level best to maneuver him into a bedroom, any bedroom, within thirty seconds of spotting his handsome face. Turning the image over in her mind, C.J. enjoyed the vision of the princely Rowan warding off Vesta's amorous advances and losing a little of that suave edge.

"Sure you're not interested in Vesta?" she asked hopefully.

"I don't think so, Clementine."

This game had gone on long enough. She snapped the peak of her cap down even farther, giving her a moment to swallow the fact that he'd called her Clementine and she didn't have any way of striking back. Rowan McKenna was one annoying man. And the only way to deal with him seemed to be to get rid of him.

Gingerly she settled herself back in her dentist's chair, folding her hands primly in front of her. "So tell me, Mr. McKenna," she said coolly. "What are you really doing in Sparks? Are you taking over Buzz's factory? Or are you just here to pester the lot of us?"

He smiled, but offered no response. Backing up enough to lounge against the door frame, he gazed at her for a long moment.

"Are you going to give me an answer?" she prompted.

He raised an eyebrow. "A better question might be why you're so darned interested."

And then he slid out the door as smoothly and quietly as he'd entered, leaving C.J. perplexed and frustrated. The man was too attractive and too high-handed for his own good—or for hers. She didn't like him or his potential as a troublemaker one bit.

She leaned all the way back in her antique dentist's chair, musing over the significance of his visit, searching for motives, clues, anything that would tell her whether he was going to pose a problem to her revenge scheme against the Farleys. But even when she replayed every bit of their conversation, she had no idea what he wanted, or what he thought he could gain.

"One good thing," she said out loud. "If I didn't get anything out of him, he sure didn't get anything out of me, either."

It was a comforting idea. Slowly, she expelled a breath. "Well, Mr. Prince of Takeovers," she announced, gazing up at her "woman scorned" sampler. "I think I'd call this round a draw."

THWARTED. Rowan scowled as he hiked down the gravel driveway from her funky little office building, making his way back to his rental car. At the moment, he was feeling thwarted, frustrated and very irritated.

And it was C. J. Bede's fault.

All he'd wanted was a little information from the one person he'd run across who was not in Buzz Farley's pocket, who might be objective. But she had brushed him off like a fly.

Rowan McKenna wasn't accustomed to being treated like a fly.

As a matter of fact, he was usually very good with potential sources of information—especially female ones. "How did he do that?" his friends and enemies whispered every time he pulled off a delicate deal. "Does he have ESP or what?"

But Rowan never told his secrets. He just reaped the benefits of the best background data on Wall Street. It wasn't any kind of psychic ability, and certainly not insider tips. Nope. It was instinct, with some help from cold, hard facts.

Unfortunately, he hadn't gotten even one fact out of C. J. Bede. Was he losing his touch?

Blasting out of her driveway, Rowan tightened his fingers on the steering wheel, still itching to go back there and pull off that damn baseball cap and see for himself what she was hiding. At least that way he'd see her eyes.

He narrowed his gaze at the empty road ahead of him. There was something about her. Something he couldn't quite put his finger on. Something not quite right. And yet very intriguing...

"McKenna, you've been on the road too long," he muttered. He knew what the trouble was, and it wasn't that C.J. was intriguing. It was just that she was *different*. Everyone else in town had been fawning all over him, while she hadn't even bothered to be polite. "When one snippy little woman piques your interest just because she doesn't play the game your way, it's time to hang it up. A vacation isn't what you need, buddy."

After years of eighteen-hour workdays, spending his evenings immersed in black coffee and vending machines instead of the champagne and caviar everyone assumed, he was just plain tired. His friends, his doc-

Park, maybe she'd like a remodeled barn in the wilds of Wisconsin.

His smile widened. It was worth a try. And it would also bring him smack-dab into the line of C. J. Bede's fire, which sounded like a whole lot of fun at the moment.

"I always did like a challenge," he said lightly.

After all, who was C. J. Bede to hold out against the Prince of Takeovers?

Chapter Two

Rousing herself from dangerous thoughts about Rowan McKenna, C.J. headed out the door and across the lawn to her barn of a house. Her first renovation project, the barn was all soaring beams, golden oak woodwork and sun-splashed open spaces. With so many windows and skylights, it was a bear to keep heated, but C.J. didn't care. She loved her barn.

The decor was country primitive mixed with art deco and a few pieces of pop art, and she loved that, too. Her mother was one of the only people besides her customers who'd seen the inside of C.J.'s home. Mama felt it was too Spartan, too plain, too all-around weird for a normal girl. But C.J. wouldn't budge. She wouldn't add or change a thing.

As she let herself in the front door, her gray cat, a tabby named Samantha, looked up casually, but didn't bother to get up and greet her owner. "Spoiled cat," C.J. muttered.

But she bent down to scratch her furry pal, none-theless. Except for Miss Prudence Hopmiller, who lived next door, Samantha was C.J.'s best friend.

After giving the purring cat a final pat, C.J. dashed into the shower. On the way, she caught sight of herself in the mirror and immediately wished she hadn't looked. Her face was filthy, her nose was sunburned and her hair had definitely seen better days. Lifting a limp strand, she concluded it was a good thing she'd had it stuck under a hat when she saw Rowan.

"Oh, pooh," she told her unkempt reflection. "He didn't care what you looked like. He didn't even notice you were a woman."

That thought only made her feel worse, and she jumped into the shower before she had a chance to dwell on it. Racing in and out in ten minutes flat, she quickly changed into clean clothes, in a rush to be on time for dinner at Miss Prudence Hopmiller's house. It was a standing invitation—they ate together promptly at six o'clock every Wednesday and Sunday night—and C.J. knew better than to show up at Miss Pru's with smudges on her nose *or* her clothes.

As she tucked a loose white blouse into a clean pair of jeans, she hurriedly set out some treats for Samantha and looked around for her shoes. She was always very punctual, and the fact that she was running late was making her crazy. She hated feeling so scattered, so out of control.

It was all Rowan McKenna's fault. If he hadn't gotten her all agitated, making her lose track of the time, she wouldn't have been behind schedule.

"Dadblast the Prince of Takeovers, anyway," she swore loudly, scaring Samantha, who went streaking up the stairs.

Twisting her hair into a wet braid, C.J. stuck a rubber band on it, and then finally headed over to

Miss Pru's. Although she lived less than half a mile away if you cut across the field, C.J. took her car, whipping up the gravel driveway and spinning to a stop outside the door.

A bit of a monstrosity, the Hopmiller house featured a weather-vaned cupola rising from the roof and lots of frilly ironwork trim. It had been quite the grand abode in its day, and it still looked pretty good, considering the house had celebrated its hundredth birthday twenty years ago. Some people said Miss Pru had already been old by the time the house was built, that the old lady was a witch who'd lived forever, but C.J. knew better. Miss Pru wasn't a day over ninety. Well, ninety-five, anyway.

"Good gracious!" Miss Pru exclaimed as she held open the screen door for C.J. "You are in a bustle today, aren't you, Clementine? Why, you must have been traveling over thirty miles an hour!"

C.J. smiled. Miss Pru probably hadn't driven a car since 1935. Thirty miles an hour must sound like the speed of light to her. But then, being around Miss Pru was always entertaining. She might be getting on in years, but she was every inch a lady, from her careful coiffure to the high lace collar of her blouse. Miss Pru was petite, but she had an ingrained sense of presence and style that made her seem larger than life.

As C.J. followed obediently, Miss Pru led the way back to the dining room, where she'd already brought out the good china and set the table, complete with polished silver candlesticks and heavy old-fashioned flatware. After signaling to C.J. to be seated, Miss Pru sat herself down carefully at the head of the table.

"So, my dear," she said grandly, gazing down the length of the table. "Who was that young man, and why did he leave your office in such a dither?"

C.J. felt her mouth fall open. "I—I don't know what you mean—"

"Now, Clementine, there's no point in being coy. I saw your young man, with my very own opera glasses," Miss Pru returned calmly. "I like to keep an eye on you. I climb up to the cupola, where I can get a clear view right to your front door."

"Are you saying you climb up on the roof?"

Miss Pru carefully removed the cover from a silver serving dish. "There is a staircase, my dear. And I only go up when I hear someone come down the road and turn into your driveway."

C.J. was astonished. She had a spy next door, and she'd never realized. "Miss Pru, are you telling me that every time I have a customer, or anybody at all dropping by my office, you watch us through binoculars?"

"Well, usually, as soon as I see who it is, I put down my glasses and leave you to your privacy. But this young man seemed rather troubling." Miss Pru shook her head sagely, barely ruffling the soft white strands of her upswept hairdo. "This gentleman was a different kettle of fish altogether. I was a bit concerned when I saw him go in, so I kept up my surveillance until I was sure he'd departed. But, my heavens, Clementine, he stomped out of there as mad as the proverbial wet hen."

"He did?" C.J. couldn't hold back a satisfied smile. So the cool-as-a-cucumber Prince of Takeovers hadn't been able to hang on to his cool.

"Well, not exactly like a wet hen," Miss Pru hedged. "Perhaps I should say he was all aflutter. No, no, that's not it, either. When one sees such a dark scowl on such a handsome face, it's rather hard to describe."

C.J. made a point of serving herself a slice of roast beef from the meat platter. "What a lovely dinner," she said with enthusiasm. "You must have been cooking all day, Miss Pru."

"As you very well know, Mayetta Smalls comes in to cook for me, and I don't even enter the kitchen." Miss Pru gave C.J. a severe look. "Now stop trying to distract me. I want to know who that attractive young man was, and I want to know why he left under such a thundercloud."

"Attractive?" Pretending to be surprised, C.J. speared a carrot and chewed thoughtfully. "Did you think he was attractive? I didn't really notice."

Miss Pru's lips pressed into a disapproving line. "You could hardly have failed to notice, my dear."

"I didn't. Really."

"If you didn't, it's only because you were trying very hard not to." The elderly woman leaned forward eagerly, completely ignoring her dinner. "Why are you so all-fired set on paying no attention to a hunk like that one?"

C.J. almost choked on her carrot. "Hunk? Where did you learn a word like that?"

"I've started watching the soap operas," Miss Pru announced brightly. "I just love that 'Hope Springs Eternal.'"

"Oh, Miss Pru . . ."

Her soft gray eyes twinkled as she gave C.J. an encouraging look. "He isn't *the one,* is he?"

"The one *what?*"

"The one for you. Even I know that when you meet *the one,* you will immediately recognize him."

"Miss Pru, can we not talk about Rowan McKenna anymore?" C.J. pleaded.

"He has a sterling name, doesn't he?" her ninety-year-old nemesis persisted. "Rowan McKenna. Yes, I like that. So what is it exactly about him that's causing all this fuss?"

There was no way around it. She was going to have to offer some sort of explanation, or Miss Pru would be on it like a terrier with a bone. "It's just that..."

"Yes?"

"Well, he might be a bit of a problem, professionally. I'm not sure, mind you," she added vaguely, "but there's a rumor that he might be thinking of interfering with some plans I have."

"What sort of plans?"

"Nothing important," she said quickly. There was no way in the world she was going to tell kind, sweet old Miss Pru the gruesome details of her revenge scheme. Somehow, she didn't think Miss Pru would be happy to hear that she'd been feeding tea and sympathy to a vengeful, vindictive troublemaker all these years.

"Hmm." Her friend's eyes crinkled as she pondered the problem. "He did look like a very resolute sort of person. I can see where he might pose a certain amount of difficulty. But you know, my dear, you can charm a bee more easily with honey than with vinegar."

"Excuse me?"

"It seems to me that if you truly want to neutralize your Mr. McKenna, using a little charm might be in order."

"Charm? Me?" C.J. asked doubtfully.

"Well, of course, Clementine." Daintily Miss Pru touched her napkin to the corners of her mouth. "If you set your mind to it, my dear, I wouldn't be a bit surprised to see you wrap the man around your little finger."

"*You* might not be surprised, Miss Pru..." C.J. took a deep breath, unable to even imagine charming Rowan McKenna. "But *I* certainly would."

"COME ON, ODELL, you must've heard something by now." C.J. stopped pacing long enough to spear the editor of the Sparks *Sentinel* with a lethal glare. "A man like that doesn't hang around a town like this one without somebody knowing something."

"I already told you, C.J. He's a slick one. Everybody says he's right friendly, but nobody knows why he's here or what he's aimin' for." Odell Watson smoothed a hand over the top of his bald head as he leaned all the way back in his creaky wooden chair. "Way I figger it, that McKenna fella is snoopin' for dirt on the Farley place, seeing if there's anything there worth takin' over. He must've spent an hour talking to Florette over at the Five-and-Dime, and you know Florette. Can't hardly shut her up. She told him all he cared to know and then some, unless I miss my guess."

C.J. hid a smile. Rowan McKenna sifting through one of Florette Bunch's long-winded monologues was a scene she was sorry she'd missed.

"So," Odell continued, pulling on his suspenders importantly, "your Mr. McKenna probably knows everything there is to know about Sparks by now, name, rank and serial number included."

Her smile slid into a frown. "That doesn't sound good," she muttered. She didn't welcome the idea of the nosy Mr. McKenna peeking into her own family secrets, or putting two and two together on the subject of the disintegrating fireworks factory and who was behind its rapid decline. "Not good at all."

"Ahem," Odell said meaningfully. "C.J....?"

"What?" she asked impatiently, still lost in her thoughts. But Odell didn't answer, forcing her to turn back around to see what he wanted.

Holy smokes. *Him.* She blinked, thinking there was must have been some mistake. But no, Rowan McKenna was still there, big as life, grinning at her like a possum, lounging next to the front window of the newspaper office. C.J.'s blood began to dance the tango in her veins.

"Hi," he said cheerfully.

"Go away," she returned without thinking. It was more of a plea than an order.

The way C.J. remembered it, they'd parted under less than friendly circumstances. How had Miss Pru described it? Something about a dark scowl on a handsome face. Well, there was no sign of a scowl now.

She snapped down the peak of her baseball cap and glared at him. She just couldn't help it. He truly brought out the surly side of her.

"Hey there, Mr. McKenna," Odell offered, sending curious glances between the two of them. Stepping into the conversational breach, Odell gabbed away, yanking on his suspenders every once in a while for emphasis. "So, Mr. McKenna, you hankering to look at some back issues of the *Sentinel,* maybe? We don't keep them microfilms like you city folk are used to, but you're welcome to take a gander at the old papers in the basement, if a few spiders won't run you off."

Odell smiled broadly, overplaying the country bumpkin bit outrageously, but Rowan didn't seem to notice. He was too busy watching C.J. while she made a point of staring at his shoes. Tasseled loafers. "I should've known," she murmured.

"Thanks for the offer, Mr. Watson," McKenna said in that charming, oozy voice of his. "But I came by to see C.J."

His gaze didn't waver, and neither did hers. If only she could guess what he wanted with her, and why just the sight of him gave her the willies. With him in the room, her face felt flushed, her stomach fluttered, her toes tingled and she couldn't seem to stand still. It was like having the flu. The Rowan McKenna Flu.

"Now why in the world would you come to the newspaper to see me?" she demanded. Her hands were waving in the air when she talked, something she never did, so she pushed them into the pockets of her denim jacket before anyone noticed. "I don't hang out at the *Sentinel* as a rule."

"I saw you," he said calmly, inclining a thumb at the large plate-glass window that looked out onto Main Street. "I happened to be walking by and I saw you inside talking to Mr. Watson, and I decided this was my chance."

"Chance for what?" C.J. asked suspiciously, as Odell began to surreptitiously take notes. Taking notes? What in heaven's name was that all about?

Squinting over his shoulder, she could make out "Hotshot woos local lovely..." "Oh, for heaven's sake," she muttered. "Odell, stop that this instant." But he kept on writing.

All she needed was for some bogus item about her and the Prince of Takeovers to show up in tomorrow's "Tattler" column. Odell loved to throw out little tidbits to get things stirred up in Sparks. Not that anyone in town would recognize C. J. Bede as the "local lovely" in question.

Ignoring Odell for the moment, she shifted her focus back to Rowan McKenna. "What do you want?" she asked him again.

"Ice cream," Rowan said gallantly, offering an arm. "My treat, of course."

C.J. bit her lip. Not once in her entire life had any member of the male population of Sparks treated her to a cone at the Double Dipper across the street. Finally, after all these years, an eligible man was asking her to share ice cream with him in full view of the town, and she couldn't do it. Not when she suspected he had ulterior motives, when she couldn't trust him as far as she could throw him.

"Why?" she asked flatly.

He raised a dark eyebrow. "Do I need a reason to ask a beautiful woman to spend a little time with me?"

She sent a glance down at her wrinkled chambray shirt and dusty jeans. "Beautiful woman, my foot." Head high, jaw clenched, she strode for the front door, turning back to announce, "All you're looking for is a load of gossip from the town rebel. Well, I'm not spilling my guts, not for a lousy ice-cream cone."

"I don't get it," she heard McKenna mutter behind her. "I've never had this much trouble with a woman. Why does she dislike me?"

"C.J. ain't no woman," Odell Watson cackled. "More nearly a wildcat, if you ask me."

Ears burning, C.J. kept walking, out the door and down Main Street. She was proud to be a wildcat, she told herself firmly. She didn't need anything or anybody, especially not Rowan McKenna or his tasseled loafers or his worthless ice-cream offers.

As if her day weren't bad enough, she caught sight of Karla and Darla Farley dead ahead. A contrast of country-club tan and tennis whites, Karla was just pulling her baby blue Cadillac convertible, license plate FARLEY 3, in front of a fire hydrant, with her sister Darla, also in tennis clothes, perched in the passenger seat. The two of them were squabbling about something—nothing new there—as the gigantic car lurched to a sideways stop and they both popped out, completely ignoring the hydrant.

All she needed to really blow her temper sky-high was a run-in with them. Quickly, C.J. changed direction, ducking into the alley next to the Five-and-Dime. She was safely out of view, but she could still hear their high-pitched voices as they shouted at each other. None of the Farleys knew the meaning of the word *quiet,* and certainly not these two.

"I already told you," Karla bellowed. "I get first dibs."

"You do not!" Darla squealed back at her. "Who died and made you king, anyway? You always try to run everyth—"

"He's mine, do you hear? Mine!"

As C.J. lurked in the alley, she heard an abrupt shift in the tone of their voices. Suddenly the strident, unpleasant mood evaporated into the hazy summer air.

"Why, it's Rowan," Karla said languorously, dripping snake oil with every syllable.

And C.J. knew with dreadful certainty what the Farley girls' latest battle was about. They both wanted a shot at Rowan McKenna. And like a lamb led to the slaughter, he'd chosen that moment to walk down Main Street.

"Hi, Rowan," they cooed in unison.

"Hello, ladies."

C.J. was happy to note a definite chill in his words. Curiosity got the best of her; she couldn't resist seeing for herself what was going on. As various townspeople passed by, all happy to eavesdrop on anything that smacked of good gossip, C.J. crossed her arms and leaned against the wall of the Five-and-Dime, trying to fade in with the worn bricks.

Darla and Karla had the man surrounded, one on each arm, as they pressed their slinky bodies up against him. At this point, nobody had the advantage, especially not the poor Prince of Takeovers, who was being squished within an inch of his life.

"We just think it's *sooo* exciting to have a real celebrity like you in little old Sparks," Karla chirped, flashing Passion Pink fingernails and a whole armful of tennis bracelets.

"I hear you've been sounding people out, what they think of Sparks and all," Darla chimed in. "Anything you need to know, anything at all, you just ask us, y' hear? Why, we know everything there is to know about Sparks. Our granddaddy practically founded this town."

"Is that so?" he asked uneasily, trying vainly to disengage his arms from their grasp.

C.J. was getting a real chuckle out of his predicament, what with two clinging vines stuck to him like that. She began to feel sorry for the poor Prince. But not sorry enough to rescue him.

"I, uh, have a meeting," he said suddenly, spinning away from them and hotfooting it away from their clutching fingers.

He was headed straight for C.J. And she couldn't sneak back into the alley, either, because Becky Lee Smalls and her baby carriage had moved in behind her, cutting her off. Her only chance to escape was to veer in the other direction and get out of sight as quickly as possible. That meant heading right inside Petticoat Junction, Sparks's one and only ladies' apparel boutique.

She cringed as the little bells on the door tinkled, announcing her arrival. Out of the frying pan and into the fire. It was irrational and silly, but C.J. hated Petticoat Junction with every fiber of her being. It stood for all that was superficial and dumb about being a woman, all the things she wasn't. With ruffles and lace everywhere, it was definitely not her kind of place.

C.J. glanced around at the racks of drippy dresses and polyester separates with ill-concealed distaste. But then Rainy Day Delmar, the oldest Delmar girl and the only clerk at Petticoat Junction, came sliding up. Rainy Day was pretty enough, but she seemed to be going through one of those awkward teenage stages where attitude was everything. As usual, she was wearing a sulky expression with her miniskirt.

"So," the girl said suspiciously, obviously surprised to see C.J. in her store. "Can I help you or something?"

"Just looking." Grabbing whatever was handy, C.J. feigned interest in a display of fancy dinner dresses. They were hideous, erupting sequins and beads from every seam, and it was tough going to even pretend to be momentarily interested. Intent on putting on a good show, she nabbed the nearest gown in her size and held it up to her body. It was a star-spangled monstrosity, complete with big red-sequin stars over the breasts and royal blue fringe on the shoulders.

"Like, it's none of my business," Rainy Day interrupted, casting an eye at the dress. "But you aren't planning on entering the Miss Firecracker pageant, are you?"

C.J.'s mouth fell open. No one had ever put her and the annual Miss Firecracker pageant in the same sentence. "Excuse me, Rainy Day, but I think you've mistaken me for someone else."

"Just don't enter, okay?" the girl pleaded.

"Me?" she asked, trying not to laugh. "In a beauty pageant?"

Rainy Day looked as if she was about to burst into tears as she pointed to the evening gown C.J. was holding. "Then what about that?"

"Rainy Day," she said patiently, "I'm too old and too crotchety to be twirling batons or singing 'God

Bless America' in some dippy pageant. Take a look at me, Rainy Day. What were you thinking?''

"Well, I did think it was goofy, seeing as how you're kind of old." The girl chewed on her fingernail. "But you do have a good figure for the swimsuit competition, what with, like, cleavage and stuff. And that dress would really look great on you." She sighed heavily. "I'm, like, way too short for it, even though it's perfect. For the judges, I mean, seeing as how it's red, white and blue, and they really go for that patriotic stuff."

"I'm sure it would look much better on you than me," C.J. said with enthusiasm, handing over the awful dress. She suppressed a smile. Imagine, Rainy Day being afraid of competition from *her*. There was a first time for everything, she supposed.

Now that she had her dress, Rainy Day was willing to be magnanimous. "You know," she said, cocking her head as she looked C.J. up and down with a practiced pageant eye, "you could really wipe up in the evening-gown competition, if you fixed up your hair and stuff. Have you ever thought about entering?"

"Thanks, but no thanks," C.J. said quickly, just as the front door tinkled, announcing new arrivals. Once she heard the voices, C.J. knew her luck had run out. Karla and Darla were squeezing themselves into petticoat Junction, and there was no escape, no back door, no place to hide.

"Well, my, my. If it isn't Clemmy Bede," Karla declared, flashing a big, cheesy smile that sparkled almost as much as her tennis-racket-shaped diamond earrings. "If I were you, Rainy Day, I'd tell her she has to wash up before she can handle the merchandise. Nobody else in town is going to want to try on *soiled* things.''

Before she hauled off and hit Karla, C.J. reached blindly for a dress. ''Where's the try-on room?'' she asked, glancing down at the purple strapless number over her arm. ''This one looks like just what I need.''

Rainy Day pointed out the room, behind a nearby curtain, as Darla planted her hands on her hips and demanded, ''And why is *she* looking at evening dresses?''

''Well,''·Karla said with a snorting laugh, ''we know it's not for the Firecracker Ball, now don't we? 'Cause certain people are not invited to country-club functions, now are they?''

''It's not for the Miss Firecracker pageant, either,'' Rainy Day put in helpfully. ''I already asked.''

Darla smirked. ''What's it for, Clemmy?''

''None of your business.'' C.J. picked up the dress, and two or three more for good measure, and swept into the small try-on cubicle. She had no intention of answering their questions, or standing around fighting with them, either.

As she hung up the dresses, C.J. realized there was one good thing about these constant confrontations with her wicked stepsisters. It made C.J. even more determined to have her revenge, to see the entire Farley family destitute and begging for mercy.

''No mercy,'' she whispered, sitting down on the cushy little stool in the corner. ''Not one drop.''

As usual, the twins were incapable of keeping their voices down, even though they knew their mortal enemy was within range. ''I get him,'' Darla insisted loudly, and C.J. shook her head. Still battling over

Rowan McKenna, as though he would ever be interested in either of them.

"Daddy says one of us has to marry him," Karla hissed. "And I have a better chance."

Marry him? Could ol' Buzz Farley possibly be deluded enough to think he could marry off one of his awful daughters to someone like Rowan McKenna? C.J. moved a little closer to the door of the dressing room, trying to hear better.

"One of us has to marry him to keep the fireworks factory in Farley hands," Karla went on, making no attempt to be quiet about this idiotic plan. "And it's going to be me."

"But he's ignoring us," Darla whined. "If you're going to marry him, he's got to pay attention sooner or later."

"Good point," C.J. said under her breath.

"Oh, Darla, sometimes you are so *thick*. We're the Dance Committee for the Firecracker Ball, aren't we?"

"Of course," Darla shot back. "We're always the Dance Committee."

"Right." Karla dropped her voice to a heavy whisper that C.J. could still hear perfectly. "Daddy already invited Rowan to the ball, and he already said yes."

"But just because he's at the ball doesn't mean he'll pay any attention."

"Oh, yeah?" Karla taunted. "And what about his half of the bottle rocket? Everyone invited gets one, you know."

C.J. tried not to giggle. They gave them a *what?* A half a bottle rocket? Trust the owners of a firecracker factory to come up with party favors that dopey.

"And you know what happens next, now don't you, Darla?" Karla asked snidely.

"Sure," her sister responded dreamily. "The guy has to find the girl with the other half of his rocket and they dance together, the first and last dances. Do you remember Ronny Plunkett? His rocket fitted my rocket, and it was so romantic."

"Darla, you are such a fool. Of course his rocket fitted your rocket. You cheated!"

"It was not cheating," Darla said testily. "I just had to make sure he was mine all night, that's all."

"I don't care what it was. It was a good idea, and I'm going to do it again."

"Oh. But Ronny's not coming. He moved to Green Bay, Karla."

"Not Ronny, you idiot! I'm cheating to make sure *Rowan McKenna* gets the other half of *my* bottle rocket." Karla's voice rose with enthusiasm. "So when he comes to the ball, he has no choice. He dances with me, he pays attention to me and he falls in love with *me*. Hook, line and sinker."

"What about me?" Darla wailed.

"I don't care!" Karla shouted back. "It's too late—I already did it, and he's getting the other half of *my* rocket!"

As they kept on squabbling, C.J. sat in her dressing room, considering the possibilities. What if she, too, put in an appearance at the Firecracker Ball? She wouldn't be invited, of course, but there were ways around that, like stealing an invitation. It was a masquerade, so no one would notice one extra woman, as long as she had an invitation.

And once she'd committed that bit of thievery, why not go ahead and steal the other half of Rowan McKenna's bottle rocket, so *she'd* be the one he danced with, not Karla?

She smiled wickedly. *"You can charm a bee more easily with honey than with vinegar,"* Miss Pru had said. And then there was Rainy Day's comment. *"You could really wipe up in the evening-gown competition, if you fixed up your hair and stuff."*

So what if Clementine Jemima Bede staged her own evening-gown competition, showing up at the Firecracker Ball dressed to kill, hidden behind a mask and fancy clothes?

She could definitely put a crimp in Karla and Darla's matrimonial plans. But could she also charm some answers out of the Prince of Takeovers?

Chapter Three

"This is a terrible idea," she told herself, blowing the words out the window of her pickup truck. "The worst idea I've ever had."

So why was she practically giggling with glee? It *was* terrible. It was also wicked, dishonest, mean-spirited and downright sneaky, but deep down, Clementine Jemima Bede was positively in love with this idea.

It sounded so simple, so elementary that she had to keep reminding herself it wasn't going to be easy at all to slip an invitation and a bottle rocket right out from under the collective Farley noses. But if she wanted to foil the Gruesome Twosome's matchmaking scheme, that was exactly what she needed to do.

So far, so good. After dumping the pile of dresses, she'd managed to slip out of Petticoat Junction without the twins noticing. Well, that was less skill than human nature, really, since the Farley girls were still going at it hammer and tongs. They wouldn't have noticed if P. T. Barnum and his whole circus had paraded through the store.

Once she got past them, C.J. hotfooted it to her truck and roared into action. Now, as town receded behind her, she steered with one hand and dialed the Farley home with the other, thanking her lucky stars she'd put a phone in the pickup.

"Hello," somebody said faintly.

"Mim?" C.J. asked, pretty sure it wasn't the twins' mother, but not sure who else it could be.

"No, Mrs. Farley's not here," the other person returned. "There's no one here but me. This is Mayetta Smalls."

Mayetta came from one of the fourteen or fifteen branches of Smalls who lived in and around Sparks. C.J. had no idea which branch; there were far too many Smalls for anyone to keep track. Mayetta did household work for a few of the town's best families, including cooking for Miss Pru several times a week, and C.J. really ought to have figured the Farleys would be on the list. Well, there was nothing to be done about it now. Just like the rest of them, Mayetta was going to have to vacate the family home so C.J. could get in there and commit burglary.

Improvising quickly, C.J. said, "I'm calling from the factory. Mr. Farley has had an, um, accident at work."

"An accident? Oh, dear."

"Don't worry, it's nothing bad," she said quickly. "It's just . . . his pants. He split 'em." She tried not to cringe even as she said it. "He needs another pair right away. Do you think you can find some and bring them to the fireworks factory? I wouldn't ask, but he's sort of uncomfortable without any pants."

"I'll be right there," Mayetta assured her.

"Phase one complete," C.J. declared as she switched off the phone, feeling a twinge of guilt for

sending Mayetta on a wild-goose chase. But C.J. reminded herself that she was on a mission, and she
didn't have time to worry about minor inconven-
iences to innocent bystanders. "I'll give her a nice
Christmas present care of Miss Pru," she whispered.
The important thing was that the house was now
empty.

It wasn't long before she spotted Mayetta, driving
the opposite direction in a beat-up Ford. Looked as if
her plan of deception and thievery was going
smoothly, at least as far as Mayetta was concerned.
The maid would be busy for a good half hour, running back and forth to the factory.

Now all C.J. had to do was slip into the Farley place
and snoop around until she found the box of invitations and the bottle-rocket party favors. Any invitation would do, but she had to steal the right rocket—
the one that matched Rowan's. Finally she had to get
out of the Farley place alive, leaving Karla, Darla,
their mother Mim, their father Buzz and everybody
else none the wiser.

"I can do it," she said bravely, stashing her truck
behind a bush not far from the road. "Piece of cake."

Nonetheless, her heart was hammering as she edged
carefully around the trees and then sneaked up the
lawn, circling closer and closer to the palatial house.
Actually, it looked more like a tacky version of Tara
from *Gone with the Wind,* but the Farleys thought it
was very grand, with its fat white columns and trailing ivy.

C.J. had been in the place exactly once, when she
was sixteen, and the entire high school had been invited to a blowout birthday party for the twins. They'd

been their usual charming selves, while C.J. had taken one look at the man she'd just discovered was her real father and gotten rip-roaring drunk for the first and only time in her life. Ricky Smalls, who was at that time Darla's steady boyfriend, came on to C.J. in a major way, and she responded by tossing her cookies down the front of Ricky and all over the Farley lawn.

Just looking at that same manicured lawn, with its overflowing peony bushes and prize roses, C.J. wanted to retch all over again. But she had better things to do this time.

There was no sign of the baby blue Cadillac, or any of the other Farley vehicles, so C.J. figured she was still safe. But she knocked on the door, just to be sure. No answer.

She rang the doorbell, loud. No answer.

She rang it again. The peals of the bell echoed throughout the house. But there was still no answer.

"Now or never," she told herself. Taking a deep breath, she looked both ways and then tried the knob on the front door. Open. She knew it had to be. Nobody in Sparks ever locked their doors.

Once inside every footfall sounded horribly loud, and every breath she took echoed in her ears. But she made herself ignore the enormity of what she was doing and press on, looking for boxes of invitations and bottle rockets.

After determining that there was nothing of interest in the gloomy front hall, she set to work on the right side of the house, looking for signs of Firecracker Ball paraphernalia. But there was nothing out of order in the dining room, the living room or the kitchen. Either the Farleys were neater than she thought, or Mayetta had already cleaned those rooms.

"Damn," she swore under her breath. Her watch told her she'd already been in the house for ten minutes, and she was getting more nervous by the second. Who knew how much time she had, or which member of the family would wander in first?

C.J. raced through the kitchen and circled around to the other side of the house, pushing open doors and looking for something—anything—that would lead her to her invitation and her bottle rocket. But as she made her way toward the front of the house, all she hit was a walk-in pantry and what must have been Buzz's study. His desk was overflowing with graphs and charts about how terrible business was at the factory. Too bad she didn't have time to examine those in more depth.

By the time she tried the last door on the first floor, she was beginning to think she wasn't ever going to find anything. It was a sitting room of some kind, with lots of white wicker and heavily flowered chintz. She could just imagine Karla and Darla and their odious mother, Mim, lounging on all that chintz, pointing out cobwebs to Mayetta.

But it definitely looked like the kind of room where the terrible twins would pore over the invitations to the ball. And there were a couple of likely-looking cardboard boxes pushed over to one wall, too. C.J. hurried to flip open the top on the first box.

"Bingo," she said with satisfaction. It was full of creamy vellum invitations, jumbled together with envelopes, a handwritten list of society folks from near and far who were considered chic enough to be invited, and a collection of miniature bottle rockets decorated in red, white and blue. She examined one of the tiny rockets, and she had to admit they were pretty clever. The colors and the shapes varied slightly, and they'd been hand cut, with different jagged edges and notches left. This way, each one pulled apart like a small puzzle, only fitting back together with its other half.

Next she turned to the invitations. "Be our guest!" the cards proclaimed in a fancy engraved scroll. "Thirty-seventh Annual Firecracker Ball, 8 p.m. on the evening of July 1, St. Andrews Golf and Tennis Club."

It was no trouble at all to snare one, and a blank envelope, and to stick them both securely inside her jacket pocket. Part one complete. But what about the bottle rocket?

Only a few of the envelopes had already been addressed and stuffed, and Rowan's was one of them. She prodded his envelope between her fingers. Yes, it definitely felt as if it had something inside it. With her precious seconds ticking away with every heartbeat, she threw caution to the wind and ripped open the envelope, removing his invitation and a small tissue-wrapped bundle. Well, she had his half of the party favor in the palm of her hand, but where was the matching other half?

"Karla's invitation," she whispered. "It'll be in Karla's."

But even as she flipped through the other envelopes in the box, she realized there was none addressed to Karla, or Darla either, for that matter. So where was the other half of Rowan's rocket? All she could think of was that Karla had hidden the other half away somewhere, keeping it safe until the night of the ball.

"Wait," she said suddenly, struck with inspiration. "It doesn't matter! I don't have to match the one Karla gave him. I'll just give him a new one!"

As easily as that, she tossed his original rocket—the one that fitted together with Karla's—back in the box. "This is a good one," she decided, holding up a pretty blue-and-white one that snapped together in a zigzag pattern.

Working as quickly as she could manage, she popped half of the new rocket into an envelope, tossed in an invitation and wrote "Rowan McKenna" across the front in a darned good approximation of Karla's horrible handwriting. Then she licked it and stuck it fast, placing it carefully back in the box where she'd found the first one. With the other half of the rocket securely in her pocket, C.J. raised one fist in the air, and said, "Yes!" in a spirit of triumph.

But then she heard voices. Male voices.

Holy smokes. Someone was home.

She had to get out of this place. Trying her darnedest not to make any noise, she slid the boxes back where she'd found them and then eased across the floor of the sitting room, closer to the door.

When she pressed her ear to the door, the voices came in loud and clear. The men were standing in the front hall, as nearly as she could figure. *Don't panic,* she told herself, but it was too late. Blood was pounding in her ears, and her hand trembled where it rested on the doorknob.

Blast it, C.J., get a grip! she commanded herself. She was caught behind the lines in enemy territory, like countless saboteurs before her, and she was just going to have to find a way out of it.

The pep talk worked for a few seconds, until one of the men's voices became suddenly clearer, and she panicked all over again.

Rowan McKenna was out there in the hall!

Rowan McKenna and Buzz Farley were chatting out there, as if they had all day to catch flies in the vestibule, while C.J. was trapped, like a rodent, behind the door to the sitting room. She was doomed. Dead. Up a creek. Down the tubes.

Rowan McKenna would use his damn radar and zoom right in on her hiding place. And then Buzz Farley would throw her in jail for burglary, while his horrible daughters cackled. With Rowan a witness at her trial!

So much for clever plans and perfect crimes. C. J. Bede's career as a cat burglar was being nipped in the bud. She felt like screaming.

Calm down, calm down. Hysteria wasn't helping.

"There has to be a way out of this," she whispered. "Look for a way out."

A quick glance around the room showed one window that was a possible escape route, but hope died in her breast when she got close, and she realized it had been painted shut a long time ago. Stupid Farleys, anyway.

Wiping clammy hands on the front of her jeans, she walked slowly back to the door. *It's okay,* she told herself, settling in with her ear pressed to the keyhole. *I'll just wait until they go somewhere else in the house, and then take off out the front.*

Of course, if they decided to use the sitting room, she was a sitting duck. But she'd just have to pray they went somewhere else, wouldn't she?

They talked and made idle chitchat until she wanted to scream and pound her fists on the wall, but there was nothing she could do but wait. Finally, when her whole body was twisted and stiff from crouching by the door, the two men ambled away from the front hall. And headed directly for her.

Oh, no! She squeezed her eyes shut and held her breath, expecting the worst. The footsteps got louder, and so did the voices. They had to be right next to her, separated only by the thin wooden door.

But then she heard their voices again, farther down the hall this time, and she knew they'd passed her by. With a huge but silent sigh of relief, she slid a hand over her forehead. They'd passed her by!

The door to Buzz's study creaked open, and the footsteps strode right in. This was her chance, and she didn't need to be told twice. After tiptoeing out through the hall and the front door, she let loose, hightailing it back down the lawn, jumping into her truck and roaring out of there like the devil himself was on her tail.

For all she knew, he was.

CAUGHT UP in the fever of a one-woman crime wave, it had all seemed so exciting. But now, after she'd had time to think about it, the idea of going to the ball was completely out of the question.

"I can't do it," she said again, louder this time. "I don't know why I ever thought I could."

"Oh, now, Clementine, let's not be negative, shall we?" Miss Prudence Hopmiller fixed her young friend with an encouraging smile. "All you need is a little confidence."

Easy for her to say. Miss Pru wasn't the one who'd committed robbery, who was faced with a fancy-dress masquerade ball when she'd never even gone to her high school prom, who was supposed to waltz right in there and act alluring to the world's most eligible bachelor.

"No," she said flatly.

"Now, now," Miss Pru continued, "you have to save the poor young man from those odious Farley girls, don't you?"

"Do I?" C.J. asked uneasily. She hadn't told Miss Pru the complete story, just that she'd "wangled" an invitation to the Firecracker Ball to keep Karla and Darla from setting a trap for Rowan.

"Of course you do. You feel the young man has potential, and you can't abandon him to those nasty schemers." Miss Pru added staunchly, "It wouldn't be right."

Neither would breaking and entering, but I already did that. Wisely she kept her mouth shut on that score.

"I'm sure if we put on our thinking caps, we'll find the solution," Miss Pru murmured. "I attended many balls and fetes in my youth—why, my come-out was the grandest party in three states. I can tell you frankly it makes no difference if you know the rules of polite society. The girl who makes the impression is the one who tosses convention to the winds. Remember Isadora Duncan, after all!"

"Who?"

"No matter," Miss Pru said. "We'll make you the belle of the ball."

But C.J. shook her head sadly. "The only kind of party I've been to are the ones where they get a keg of beer and drink out of paper cups. At a fancy ball like this, I wouldn't know how to act or how to dance or what to say." She began to pace in front of the velveteen love seat in Miss Pru's parlor, smacking her hand against the thigh of her jeans for emphasis. "And even if I somehow managed to survive a crash course in etiquette, where would I possibly find the right thing to wear? Karla and Darla and her friends have had their dresses ready for months. Florette Bunch said that Karla's wearing something created especially for her by a designer in Chicago."

"Oh, pooh." Miss Pru dismissed that objection with a wave of one dainty hand. "What designer worth his salt would waste his dresses on that awful girl? Besides, if it's only the clothes you're worried about, well, I can offer you a whole array of lovely ball gowns to choose from."

C.J. stopped. "How?" she asked.

"Young lady," her friend said in a starchy tone, "the Hopmiller family was one of the leading families in Wisconsin for generations. All those receptions and parties we attended, with a new gown for every one, and nothing has ever been thrown away. Why, there are enough fancy dresses in my attic to put the Smithsonian's costume wing to shame."

"In the attic?" She was afraid to take Miss Pru seriously. Could suitable gowns really be sitting up there waiting? "Wouldn't they be a little out of fashion?"

"Hmph," Miss Pru scoffed. "Haven't you ever heard 'everything old is new again'?"

"Excuse me?"

"Listen to me, my dear," the tiny old lady said. "I've been watching those soap operas, and their dresses don't hold a candle to any of the things I have. Why, I remember one absolutely stunning beaded georgette frock I wore to a party in honor of Scott and Zelda Fitzgerald. And then there was the white satin Lanvin gown my youngest sister Amelia wore to Franklin Roosevelt's first inauguration. Amelia was only seventeen, and such a beauty. And the gown! Straight from Paris, and simply lovely. And not so very different from the things they wear now."

"Are you sure?"

Not bothering to answer C.J.'s pesky questions, Miss Pru took her friend's hand and began to steer them both toward the stairs. "The dresses then were quite superior," she declared. "The fabrics were ever so much nicer, and of course, all handmade. We had style then, you know."

As she trailed behind the dear old lady, a tiny spark of hope began to glimmer in C.J.'s heart. "Do you really think there would be something to fit me?" *Something that isn't full of cobwebs and doesn't smell like mothballs,* she added silently.

"Why, I feel sure of it."

As Miss Pru pulled the light switch, casting a gentle glow over the assembled trunks and cases in the attic, C.J. caught her breath. There were beautifully patterned hatboxes, armoires bursting with furs, exquisite leather wardrobe cases, all just waiting to be sprung open. It was like playing dress-up in a fairy-tale castle.

"Where do we start?" she asked eagerly.

"Wherever you like," her benefactor said gaily, popping the buckles on a huge steamer trunk. The smell of roses drifted out as Miss Pru began to set aside tissue paper and sort through the trunk's contents. She held up a delicate white camisole, cocking an eyebrow at C.J. "Will you need underthings as well, my dear?"

For the first time, C.J. began to think this just might work. With Miss Pru playing Fairy Godmother, how could she lose?

ROWAN MCKENNA was dying a slow and painful death at the Firecracker Ball. Nursing a stiff drink, he made himself a solemn promise never, ever to let himself get talked into attending any small-town function held at a country club, especially ones where you had to wear masks. The place was air conditioned, but still too hot for his taste. He was sweating under the damn mask, and he couldn't stand it.

Swearing under his breath, he ripped off his black satin Zorro mask and thrust it into the pocket of his dinner jacket. These people could pretend to be in costume if they wanted to, but not Rowan McKenna.

How long did he have to hang around for the sake of politeness before he could legitimately make an exit? Surreptitiously, he checked his watch again. *Damn.* He'd only been here twenty minutes. If this was the town's big-deal social event, he had to give it at least an hour.

Buzz Farley had promised fireworks later in the evening, too, and Rowan supposed he ought to wait for them, so he could applaud politely and pretend to be impressed. But that could be hours. How in God's name was he going to last that long?

At least he had somehow dodged the bullet of having to endure the company of the Misses Farley. Karla, the more clamorous sister, had come romping up the minute he'd entered, brandishing her bottle rocket like a fencer's épée. He could've sworn she'd had brown hair the last time he saw her, but tonight her hair was a scorching shade of red.

She was wearing some concoction of sea green satin, with a sort of mermaid's tail skirt. Her half mask was the same bilious green, with fat green and gold plumes erupting from one side. He could barely look at her without wincing.

Although he'd hoped to get away unscathed, in the end, he hadn't had a choice; she'd forced him to play the game and bring out his own rocket. Reluctantly he'd fished the thing out of his pocket and let her try to match her half to his. Thank God it hadn't fitted. He was really sweating it there while she pushed and poked, bound and determined his rocket was going to mate with hers.

"It has to go," she grunted, smashing at the two clearly unmatched rocket halves, until her sister came up and shoved her aside.

"If not yours, how about mine?" Darla tossed in, wedging her own rocket piece into the fray. Darla was wearing glow-in-the-dark silver, a sort of caftan thing. It wasn't as bad as Karla's outfit, but still ... It made him dizzy to see them side by side.

And frankly, he was appalled by their behavior. They went practically ballistic when neither of their rocket pieces fitted his, screeching at each other about betrayal and double crosses, until their father, that insufferable old coot Buzz, finally intervened and pulled them away.

At that point, Rowan drew his first clear breath of the evening. Blissfully, thankfully, he was off the hook, and neither hideous Farley sister was his for the night.

He suspected there was more to that story than he knew, however, given the depth and volume of Karla's reaction when her rocket couldn't be made to match his. As a betting man, he'd wager she'd tried to cheat at the little bottle rocket game, to make sure she'd get him as her partner, and then somehow been outfoxed. So who'd outfoxed her? And why?

Rowan wandered away from the dance floor, out through French doors and onto a small terrace. At least he could breathe out here. Taking a long swallow of his Scotch, he gazed aimlessly out at the dark golf course.

Somebody was giggling out there, under the trees, and it made him feel sad and lonely to be all alone up here on the terrace. Wasn't there even one woman in Sparks who could provide good company for a few hours?

"I wonder if C. J. Bede comes to this kind of soiree," he mused out loud. "She'd stir things up."

But even as he said it, he shook his head at his own idiocy. C.J. was the most uncooperative, unpleasant young woman he'd ever met. Okay, so she was smart.

And she built great barns. But that hardly made up for the prickly-pear attitude or the chip on her shoulder.

Hell, he'd even told her she was beautiful, and she'd contradicted him! Not that he knew what she looked like, since she always hid under those damn hats. Rowan shook his head again. This town's pickings were worse than slim.

The faint rustle of slinky fabric sounded behind him, and his heart sank. Not Karla again, limping along in her mermaid monstrosity. By God, if she'd trapped him out here, he was going to murder the woman.

But as he turned, his breath caught in his throat. This was not Karla. This was . . . a vision.

She was beautiful, so beautiful that she seemed to shimmer as he gazed at her. It must just have been his imagination playing tricks on him, or the dim, romantic cast to things out here in the moonlight, but she honestly looked as if she'd been dusted with tiny sparkles.

Her hair was long and blond, full and wavy, slipping down over her shoulders, begging to be touched. Rowan jammed his free hand into his pocket before it got any ideas.

But he couldn't look away from this fairy princess who'd just swept into the Firecracker Ball, completely without warning. As she gazed at him from behind a white, cat-eyed mask, her eyes were violet blue, and her dress was simply and perfectly white. She had lovely, glowing skin, and there was a lot of it showing.

He swallowed with difficulty. His hand shook, sloshing the ice in his glass, and he set it down before he dropped it completely. Good grief. He'd never reacted like this to a woman before. It was like being sucker-punched in the gut.

He couldn't believe that dress. The skirt was full and frothy, like a ballerina's, while the bodice was molded to her rib cage, to her breasts. It looked like lingerie, like the things he'd bought for old girlfriends in fancy French boutiques. He couldn't take his eyes off it.

"Who are you?" he asked, cursing the rough catch in his voice, as if he hadn't used it in hours.

Wordlessly she smiled. And she held up half a bottle rocket.

His pulse speeded up as he found his own piece of the rocket, but there was never any doubt in his mind. It would fit. It had to fit.

He noticed that her hand trembled as much as his own as they slid the halves of the rocket together. As easily as that, the two pieces became one, and he knew he'd found the woman he'd been waiting for.

"I think this means you're mine," he murmured. And then he pulled her into his arms.

Chapter Four

"Oh, my," she whispered, forgetting to use the low, husky voice she'd been practicing as part of her masquerade. Luckily, her words were too soft to give her away. But if she didn't get a grip soon, he'd see through her disguise before the hour was out.

She was already worn to a frazzle, and she'd only just arrived. But if he kept holding her hand like that, she was afraid her fake fingernails would fall off. And if he kept staring deep into her eyes that way, she felt sure her violet-colored contact lenses would melt away, revealing the plain old hazel irises of the real C. J. Bede.

She was the one who was supposed to be doing the bamboozling and the bewitching. *She* was the one who was supposed to be making the moves. She'd envisioned a cat-and-mouse game, a few flirtatious glances, perhaps, and maybe a dance or two in the full light of the ballroom. Just enough to keep him interested and away from the Farley girls. Maybe even enough to get him to spill a secret or two.

But out here, with the two of them all alone under the moonlight... This was a whole different proposition.

Under the onslaught of his rapt gaze, she felt sure he now knew everything from the number of tiny pearls stitched to her bodice to the brand of expensive French perfume Miss Pru had lent her. Since the top of her gown was only a bustier, leaving a great deal of skin exposed, he was getting an eyeful of her measurements, too.

There were only inches separating them now, and she had no choice but to stare up into his crystal blue eyes. His eyes were a striking color—obviously the real thing—and they contrasted sharply with his thick, dark lashes.

His hard arms circled her waist, holding her fast, and she couldn't have blocked out the feel of his big handsome body all around her, so strong and so incredibly hot, even if she'd wanted to. The man felt like a furnace. She could barely breathe!

Pay no attention, she commanded herself. Thank goodness she was wearing the mask, which hid at least part of her face. She concentrated on taking steady breaths, on reclaiming some vestige of self-control.

After all, she had a mission here. Intrigue, interrogate and elude...

Eluding sounded like a good tactic right about now. She manufactured what she hoped was a sultry smile, and then slipped gently from his arms, just far enough away to get some perspective. Fanning her face with her worthless little evening bag, she saw the flicker of warmth in his eyes, and she knew she wasn't out of the woods yet.

There were certain advantages to staying out on the terrace, where the helpful shadows and misty moonlight made identifying her even more difficult. But at the moment, C.J. was willing to risk the brighter lights of the ballroom, if it meant putting a little distance between her and Rowan McKenna.

Besides, she was gaining more confidence in the quality of her disguise. No one was going to recognize her dressed up this way, least of all Rowan.

With new fingernails, contacts, mascara, eye shadow, her hair all jazzed up and curly, with skin showing that no one but her mother had ever seen, even C.J. was having trouble remembering who she was. She'd never worn clothes or heels like this before, never decked herself out in diamond bracelets and expensive perfume. And she'd never felt like a temptress before, either.

One other factor in favor of escaping inside had occurred to her—it was air conditioned in there, and maybe she'd cool off. Even if she knew her current temperature had nothing to do with the steamy July weather.

Careful to pitch her voice deeper and huskier than usual, she said, "I think we'd better go inside."

"Why?" he murmured. He raised a finger to trace the curve of her jaw, and she shivered before she could stop it. "Why spoil it?"

Getting desperate, C.J. searched for a throaty laugh. Didn't enchanting strangers always have throaty laughs? "Don't you want to join the party?"

"I'm perfectly happy with the party we're having right here."

He made a move to trap her again, but she saw it coming and sidestepped him neatly. Trying to look graceful, she backed farther away, until she was hovering near the French doors. "Things are moving a little too quickly for me, Mr. McKenna," she breathed.

"How do you know who I am?"

This time her smile was genuine. "Everyone knows who you are."

"But who are you?"

She had no intention of answering. After all, being a mystery woman was much more intriguing than any regular old person with a name. If she'd come as herself, or even invented a name and résumé, Rowan McKenna would've been interested for about five seconds. He was a mover and a shaker, a financial wizard, who'd played with all the best toys the world had to offer. Any *real* woman, no matter how beautiful, was old hat to him.

She had no illusions about her own attractions. The real Clementine Jemima Bede certainly didn't have any fatal beauty or magnetism to recommend her. But this way, wrapped in mystery and riddles, she might actually keep him on a string for the length of a whole evening.

"Tell me who you are," he commanded, advancing on her. The hot sparks in his eyes intensified, and he reached out for her. C.J. could tell by the resolute set to his chiseled jaw that this time he wasn't going to take no for an answer.

She backed a few steps farther away, opening her mouth to say something, *anything* to hold him off. But before the words were out, the French door behind her burst open, and Karla Farley blasted through.

"The party's inside, Rowan, honey," Karla cooed, pursing her lips in a coy pout. "What are you doing out here all alone?"

"I'm not alone," he returned coldly. His gaze shot straight to C.J.

Karla's brassy red head whipped around, taking in her rival for the first time. She peered into the shadows, where C.J. was trying to remain calm. All she'd need was to sweat under her mask, dissolve all of her makeup and reveal her true identity.

Karla's beady eyes narrowed, and C.J. stiffened, but there was no subsequent spark of recognition. Finally the elder Miss Farley demanded, "Who's she?" in a peeved tone.

"Why, Karla, you invited me. Don't you recognize me?" she whispered, making her words deep and slow and very torchy.

Karla ignored her, squeezing up closer to Rowan and grabbing his lapels. "Listen, Rowan," she said in a rush. "Whoever she is, it doesn't matter, because *you and I* were fated to be together tonight. What do you say we try our rockets again? We wouldn't want to waste—" she pressed one green-shadowed lid down in a meaningful wink, lowering her voice to a breathy whisper "—what could be a night you'll never forget."

C.J. had to bite down hard to keep from laughing. Karla was doing a variation of the same Marilyn Monroe voice C.J. had used! If it weren't so hilarious, it would've been tragic. Rowan didn't seem to notice the similarity, however. He was glaring at Karla, looking as if he'd like to wipe her off the face of the earth. It was a very gratifying feeling.

Detaching her fingers from his jacket, he said plainly, "Sorry, Karla, but my rocket's already been claimed."

And then he held up his half of the puzzle, turning to C.J. Once again, she picked up her cue. She slid her piece right up next to his. A perfect fit.

Karla's face flushed as scarlet as her hair. "But how?" she sputtered. "Somebody cheated!"

Rowan pointedly turned his back on Karla. As he pocketed his half of the rocket, C.J. tucked hers into the tiny silk evening bag Miss Pru had provided. Nobody was getting a chance to steal her rocket.

"A memento," he murmured just for her ears, patting the inside pocket where he'd slipped his half of the toy. And then he offered her his arm, indicating that she was the one he'd be spending his evening with. Together they slipped past Karla and swept back into the ballroom.

C.J. couldn't resist a small satisfied smile. Imagine Clementine Jemima Bede, sailing along on the arm of the high and mighty Prince of Takeovers, while Karla Farley sputtered and moaned behind them. Who would ever have imagined that?

IT WAS A GOOD THING Karla had interrupted them on the terrace, he decided darkly. Otherwise, he might've been tempted to throw caution to the winds and make love to his mystery woman right there.

The whole idea was crazy, of course. But so was everything else about this bizarre attraction.

Yes, she was beautiful, with her pale skin and her diaphanous dress. And yes, the delicate scent of her perfume was intoxicating, sweet and fragile, like old-fashioned gentility, evoking the image of elegant ladies in portraits by John Singer Sargent.

And yes, she had a certain sparkle in her extraordinary violet eyes, a sparkle that he found fascinating. But he'd met plenty of beauties in his time, lots of women with expensive perfume and droves of ladies who were so vivacious that they were bursting at the seams with life. But nobody had ever affected him the way this one did.

Why? He had no idea.

Rowan had never been a man who scrutinized his own emotions. Hell, he'd never thought he had any. But he did have instincts. And right now, every instinct he had told him *this* was the woman for him.

"Excuse me," she whispered, in that same husky voice that sent a trail of electric shocks down his spine. "I'm feeling somewhat . . . parched."

He loved the way her pretty pink lips pursed so delicately when she spoke. He found himself staring at her mouth, as gauche as a schoolboy, wondering what she'd do if he kissed her, hard and deep, the way he was dying to.

Quickly he looked into her violet eyes instead. "Would you like something to drink?"

"Yes, please," she murmured. "A glass of champagne."

"My pleasure." And then, before he could stop himself, he brought her hand to his lips and pressed a soft kiss into her palm. She trembled, and he loved the feeling that his slightest touch seemed to undo her. "Don't go away," he told her, and she smiled her assent.

As he backed away, reluctant to leave, he kept his gaze fixed on her. She was glancing lightly around the room, watching the other dancers, but not talking to anyone, anyone he might've been able to interrogate to find out who she was, or what this was all about.

Even separated from him by ten feet, and then twenty, she was still sending out some sort of siren's call, daring him to run back and grab her, to kiss her senseless, until he had satisfied the maddening, gut-deep ache he'd been feeling ever since he'd laid eyes on her.

If he didn't know better, he might've suspected this was love at first sight.

"Outrageous," he muttered under his breath. Love at first sight was for idiots, for poets and actors and other deluded types like that. Anybody who knew him would've laughed at the idea that Wall Street's most ruthless raider could fall prey to that kind of nonsense.

Absorbed in his thoughts, he almost missed the fact that he had bumped into Buzz Farley, his host at tonight's function. Bull-chested and red-faced, Buzz looked uncomfortable in his formal wear. He was a tall man, apparently too tall for an off-the-rack tuxedo. Both his sleeves and his pant legs were a little too short, exposing a flashy gold watch at his wrist and shiny patent leather shoes down below. Not exactly a portrait of high fashion.

"So, McKenna," Buzz said expansively, clapping him on the shoulder and giving him a broad smile. "You enjoying our little party?"

Rowan winced, wishing there was some way to avoid the Farleys altogether during his stay in Sparks. But they seemed to be everywhere. From what he'd gathered from his discreet inquiries, Buzz owned most of the town. And what he didn't own, he controlled. If

Rowan were to do business in Sparks, he'd end up dealing with ol' Buzz sooner or later. He preferred later.

"Nice party," he said politely.

He knew what Buzz wanted from him, and he knew Buzz wasn't going to get it. At least not yet. He hadn't made up his mind yet whether Farley Fireworks was worth the trouble to buy out.

"And are you enjoying my little town?"

"It's fine," Rowan answered, offering a tight smile. He didn't think Buzz would appreciate the truth, that spending time in Sparks was about as exciting as watching weeds grow.

So far, a couple of minor altercations with C. J. Bede had been the high points of his trip.

Until he saw the lady in white, of course. Her charms beat C.J.'s ten to one. He panicked suddenly, unreasonably afraid that she would've vanished into thin air while he shot the breeze with Buzz.

But when he gazed past Buzz's shoulder, Rowan saw that she was most definitely still there. And the swift kick of adrenaline he got just looking at her told him his crazy feelings were getting worse by the minute.

"You danced with my little girls yet?" Buzz asked heartily. "They're both dying to take a spin with you, boy. Got their hearts set on catching the eye of the Prince of Wall Street."

"Actually, it's the Prince of Takeovers."

"Uh-huh." Buzz's eyes narrowed. "You fixin' to take me over?"

"From what I hear, Buzz, your company's in a bit of trouble." Rowan smiled. "I'm not sure it's worth taking over."

The old man's face grew even redder. "Who'd you hear that from? It's a damn lie."

Rowan shrugged, edging around Buzz to order his drinks. He was wasting time talking to the old coot, time that could've been spent gazing into the captivating violet eyes of his mystery woman. Almost as an afterthought, he turned back to Sparks's most influential citizen. "You wouldn't happen to know who that woman is, would you, Buzz?"

"You better believe I know every single soul invited to my parties," Buzz declared, preening with his big-shot status. "Which girl you talking about?"

"The one in white, over there, by the pillar."

Buzz looked her over for a minute, squinted, cocked his head and then squinted again. "Skinny little thing. No, I don't believe I've ever seen her before. Partycrasher, must be. You just wait, and I'll get her kicked her out of here in two shakes. We can't be having stowaways at the country club. First thing you know, everybody in town'll be teeing up on my golf course."

"And wouldn't that be a tragedy," Rowan muttered.

"Yessir, it would." Buzz wrenched at his bow tie. "I'll straighten out that little girl's hash. Won't take but a minute."

"Leave her alone," he returned.

Buzz shook his head. "I don't believe in entertaining any uninvited little tramp who shows up at my door."

Rowan's hands closed into fists, and he had to work hard to keep himself from going for Buzz's throat.

"She had an invitation," he said coldly. "And she had the other half of my rocket."

Why he felt the need to jump to her defense, to punch Buzz in the gut for even thinking of sending her away, was beyond him. But standing there, allowing Buzz to call her a "tramp," annoyed the hell out of him. Rowan McKenna, the ice-cold Prince of Take-overs, the same guy who went out on a limb for no-body, was ready to get embroiled in a fistfight for a woman he barely knew.

For some reason, this lady's particular combination of delicate beauty and ethereal charm was bringing out the Sir Galahad side of him. Who'd ever have guessed? Not only did the Prince have a heart, but when it came to maligned mystery women, he had a major chink in his armor.

Rowan had honestly never had the time to decide what his "type" was, but he would never have chosen a small-town Cinderella in a fancy dress. He would've thought his type ran to the usual mix of sharp executives and aristocrats who'd look good on his arm at benefits and brunches. But this woman was different.

Once again, just as when he'd run into C. J. Bede, he was forced to admit that what was unusual or unfamiliar was what attracted him. Of course, this woman was nothing like C.J. And his interest in her was nothing like the minor skirmish of wills he and C.J. were involved in.

When he smiled at C.J., she scowled and walked away. But when he smiled at this lovely lady, she smiled back.

Besides, this woman touched him on a much more fundamental, more physical level. He took a quick gulp of his newly acquired Scotch, picking up the end of what Buzz was saying, something about those blasted bottle rockets.

"Now how'd she get your rocket? You'd have been a sight better off with one of my girls," Buzz said testily. "That girl ain't from around here, I'll guarantee you that. Why, you don't know who she is, what kind of people she comes from."

"Why, Buzz, she was obviously good enough to pass your daughters' rigorous standards and get invited to your party." He was confident his sarcastic tone was completely lost on Buzz. "Surely she's good enough to dance with me."

Buzz shrugged. "Maybe she's somebody's niece or out-of-town relative," he said reluctantly. "Maybe she's somebody my girls know, a sorority sister or something, who got herself a nose job and a little of that liposuction stuff. Those girls do that, you know. But she's nobody I recognize, I'll tell you that."

"Too bad." But he wasn't daunted. Before this night was over, Rowan swore he'd know the name of his mystery woman.

Before this night was over, he planned to know a lot more than that.

SHE WAS WALTZING. She didn't know how to waltz, but it didn't seem to matter. Whirling along in his strong arms, she felt as if she could've given Ginger Rogers a run for her money. Not only wasn't she even wobbling on her high heels, she hadn't broken so much as a nail, and the mighty Prince of Takeovers himself was completely fooled by her crazy masquerade.

If she'd ever envisioned one perfect, utterly romantic evening, this was it. A little champagne, a bit of flirtatious conversation and Rowan McKenna's rapt attention . . . all he had to do was smile in that slow, sexy way of his, or give her one of his melting glances, and she felt her temperature begin to rise.

Wrapped in each other's arms, they'd been dancing for hours, just swaying to the music under the glittering light from one intricate chandelier and a few well-placed candelabra.

She knew she was supposed to be pumping him for information on his takeover plans. But who had time for that when the band was playing "Cheek to Cheek" and Rowan's fingers were gently entwined in her hair, barely brushing the soft, sensitive skin on the back of her neck? All she could think of was that skin under his hand. All she could do was press closer, breathe deeper, give herself up to the music and the night and the man.

Their steps were so closely interlocked now that it was impossible to move without grazing his hard thighs. He pulled her into a turn, and her skirt swirled around her in a cloud of taffeta. The hand at her back urged her nearer, drawing her so close that his body imprinted itself on hers. She could feel the warm, hard length of him, top to bottom.

If she'd felt overheated or feverish before, now she was rapidly climbing the chart toward meltdown.

She could feel his heartbeat, as erratic as her own, and smell the fragrance of her own perfume, mixed tantalizingly with Rowan's scent. He smelled like clean

man, like starched linen, like a subtle touch of some
elegant, utterly masculine cologne. When his fingers
traced the edge of her bodice where it dipped low in
the back, dancing over her bare skin, she let out a little moan before she could stop herself.

"Don't do this to me," he said huskily, bending to
skim his lips over the pulse point behind her ear.

"Who's doing what to whom?" she asked in a
shaky voice, molding herself to him as his hot, hungry mouth etched a trail of fire down the slope of her
shoulder. His mouth felt wonderful. She felt like ice
cream, left out in the full summer sun, until it was one
oozy, sticky puddle.

Oh, Lord. This was torture. It was heaven. It was
impossible. It was bliss.

"Please," she whispered, but she didn't know if she
was begging him to go on, or begging him to stop.

Mischief and desire flamed in his clear blue eyes. He
leaned in, close enough to puff his hot breath against
her cheek. "Your voice... It does something to me. It
tempts me. It makes me want things I shouldn't have.
Do you know what I'm saying?"

Did she ever. His gaze, his hands, the single fact of
his existence did all that to her and more.

Unwilling to lose herself completely in the spell, she
squeezed her eyes shut. She hadn't meant to drive him
crazy. Or maybe she had. Everything was so mixed up,
so different from what she'd expected when she set out
to get next to Rowan McKenna for one small evening.

Even her voice had gone haywire. She couldn't seem
to make it come out any other way anymore. It now
required no effort, no deception at all, to talk in this
smoky, dark voice. In his arms, all she had to do was

open her mouth, and this whiskey-soaked siren's voice came tripping out.

"Rowan," she began. "I didn't mean . . . I didn't know..." She stopped awkwardly, trying to figure out what she wanted to say.

The music had stopped, too. She didn't know when it had drifted away, but there was no more "Fascination," no more "Stardust." Around them, she caught the vague sound of muffled conversations, and she saw a whole roomful of eyes, staring at her. Suddenly she felt like a scarlet woman, conducting her love affairs in full view of the whole country club.

She felt hot color rush to her cheeks. "Rowan, we can't do this. Not here."

"I don't care anymore," he returned roughly. And before she could protest, he swung her up into his arms and headed for the veranda.

"Wait," she tried to say, but he cut off her words, lowering his lips to hers and kissing her with a mix of arrogance and passion she had no hope of denying.

It wasn't fair. He tasted like Scotch. He tasted like forbidden fruit, like something so wild and sexy that it was against the law. He tasted unique, like Rowan himself, equal parts devastating charm and incredible nerve.

His mouth was hot and wet, demanding more from her than it was safe to give. But she found her arms twisting themselves around his neck, pulling his mouth closer and deeper, and she found herself lifting into the kiss, asking for more.

He tore himself away, breathing heavily, brushing kisses along the line of her chin, nibbling her ear, mumbling soft words she couldn't quite catch. But they were both a little shaky, more than a little out of control, and before she knew it, her cat-eyed mask had tipped to one side. Hastily she yanked it back into place over her eyes, petrified that he would see the real her and dump her out of his arms in shock.

Opening her eyes, she saw stars framing his dark head, twinkling above them in the black night. The air itself seemed heavier, steamier, pushing her into his embrace.

Was she fainting? Was she dreaming?

No, she was outside, back on the terrace, where he'd carried her in such an ungodly hurry. The sparkle of the stars...the hot, black night pressing around them...C.J. couldn't think of anything more seductive than sharing this sultry moonlight with Rowan, and she trembled inside the circle of his hard embrace.

"Only a few minutes till midnight," he reminded her. He nipped her earlobe between his even white teeth. "You'll have to take it off then, mystery lady."

"T-take it off?"

"Mmm-hmm." His lips curved in a rakish grin that took her breath away. "And if you don't, I'll take it off for you."

She had been such an idiot. She should've left long before this, while she still had a chance to make an easy getaway, before she was trapped on the veranda in the damn man's arms.

But still his arms held her fast. He closed in to launch another sensual assault, brushing the edge of the mask with his lips, whispering, "Why don't you take it off now?"

But she was saved from answering, saved by a sudden blitz of firecrackers. Over their heads, a shower of brilliant red sparks lit up the sky. It was followed by a tremendous, earth-shattering boom, and they both flinched, startled by the unexpected noise.

The red blaze was followed by blue and then green bursts of color, as fireworks exploded around them. C.J. hung on to him for dear life, feeling the echo of the explosions trip along her nerve endings.

And suddenly a whole bunch of people had crowded out onto the small terrace to get a better view, jostling her and Rowan. A man in a pale blue dinner jacket shouted, "Hey, it's midnight! Take your mask off and kiss me quick, somebody!"

A long whistle pierced the sky, followed by a flash of pink stars. The party-goers in the crowd around them tore off their masks and plastered each other with kisses under the cascading light of the firecrackers.

Rowan just stood there, staring at her expectantly, a half smile playing over his narrow lips. C.J. knew her moment of crisis was at hand.

She raised a hand, fingering the beaded curve over her cheek. If she revealed who she was, what would he do?

Would he say, *C.J., I knew it was you!* and pull her into his arms?

Don't be ridiculous, declared a nasty little voice inside her head. Abruptly, her sense of herself as a mysterious, alluring woman deserted her. In her heart, she was still plain old C.J., the town outcast, the gawky girl who was always on the outside looking in when it came to being special or beautiful or desirable.

She felt sure that if he saw the real woman under the mask, this romantic interlude would come to a screeching halt. No more sweet kisses, no more smoky glances. Just plain old horror on Rowan's face when he realized whom he'd been romancing.

Her pulse pounding, her heart breaking, C.J. raised her chin. This princess wasn't going to let her prince see her turn back into a pumpkin. "I'm sorry," she told him. "I just can't."

And before he could stop her, she wrenched away from his arms. Surprise was on her side. By the time he realized what she meant to do, she was already halfway across the ballroom.

"Wait!" he called out after her. She could hear the frustration and anger in his voice. "Wait, dammit! I don't even know your name."

But Clementine kept going. He didn't know her name, and that was exactly the way she wanted it.

Chapter Five

She felt like an escaped convict, with the blood-hounds hot on her trail. All she needed were a few spotlights and screaming sirens, and maybe a big, ugly guy with a gun.

Stop or I'll shoot!

No way! You'll never take me alive!

It was nonsense, of course, but this frantic flight across the dark golf course was playing havoc with her nerves. C.J. stopped for a breather, pulling off her mask and her high heels in the shadow of a tall oak tree.

Damn this stupid white dress. She might as well have lit signal flares to announce her location.

She peered cautiously around the tree. Was Mc-Kenna still back there? With only a few stars and a shadowy moon to guide her and the occasional showers of sparks from the firecrackers, it was hard to tell. But she thought she saw something moving, over there by the water hazard on the fourth hole. Damn the man. Why couldn't he just give up and let her escape into the night, with her dignity intact?

As she recalled the fairy tale, Prince Charming was supposed to stand there, clutching the shoe desperately. He wasn't supposed to come after her!

Maybe she should've left a shoe behind to give him something to do. Well, there was no help for it now. After all, Rowan McKenna was no Prince Charming, and he seemed determined to follow her, shoe or not.

Of course, she could've just let him catch her, told him the truth and gone on her merry way. But some stubborn streak inside her made that impossible. She simply couldn't admit to being C. J. Bede. Not to him.

"I have my pride," she muttered, and she moved out from behind her tree, ready to make her move.

By the time she'd finished tripping around the golf course, she had a stitch in her side, she was dripping with perspiration and the hot night air had gotten even stickier.

Meanwhile, she was farther away from her pickup than when she'd started. And the only direct route to her truck was through the creepy little stand of woods that bordered this side of the golf course.

She shivered. There were all kinds of bumps and holes and nasty little creatures in that woods, and she didn't want to go scrambling through it. But she didn't have a choice.

With Rowan behind her and that spooky woods in front, she was caught between the devil and the deep blue sea.

Still dangling her shoes, her evening purse and her beaded white mask, she screwed up her courage and headed for the woods. At least here, she could be pretty darn sure ol' Rowan couldn't pick up her trail. Even in a white dress, she'd be impossible to see.

Feeling her way along, she ignored all the eerie noises and funny shadows, edging forward through the darkness. If she just kept heading downhill, she felt sure she'd bump into her truck in no time. But as she kept going, and as she confronted more woods, she was afraid she was lost. Should it be taking this long?

Finally, blessedly, she saw the break in the trees she'd been waiting for, and she knew she was almost there. She ran the rest of the way, not ready to feel safe until the rusty green door of her pickup was under her fingers. Yanking open the door, she jumped in, tossing her baggage into the passenger seat. After snatching the keys out of the glove compartment, she prepared to blast out of there.

"But what if I pass someone on the road?" she asked suddenly. Anyone from town would recognize her truck in a minute. "Even driving by, they'll see the top of this dress, and everyone will know it was me who crashed the ball."

She paused, wondering if she dared waste any more time trying to cover up her party attire. "I don't have a choice," she decided, taking the time to rustle around in the back of the truck. Luckily she found a paint-spotted work shirt and a crumpled baseball cap, both left there weeks ago. With the shirt buttoned on over her strapless dress, she was at least fairly normal from the waist up.

"I just better not have an accident," she grumbled, imagining some good citizen of Sparks pulling her out of the truck and finding her tutu poking out from under the chambray shirt. Tucking the extra folds of fabric under her knees, she decided she would simply drive *very* carefully.

Twisting the rearview mirror around, C.J. shuddered at her own reflection. Her hair was limp and littered with leaves, her face was pale and dirt streaked and she looked as if she'd just been through the camping trip from hell.

There was no way anyone in the world would connect this disheveled ragamuffin with the elegant princess who'd whirled on the dance floor in Rowan McKenna's arms. That should have meant success. So why did the thought depress her so much?

"Get over it," she muttered, brushing out the leaves and sticking her hair up underneath the trusty baseball cap. As she wrenched off her fake fingernails and then rubbed the vestiges of her makeup off with a tissue, she told herself, "You were never meant to be the belle of the ball, and you'll never be again, so you might as well get used to being plain old C.J."

Determined to put tonight and its crazy events out of her mind for good, she tossed the fingernails and the tissue onto the seat along with her shoes and the other bits of her disguise. Then she fired up the old Ford and pulled out onto the narrow gravel road.

She'd gone no more than a mile when she saw a flash of white and a sudden flicker of motion up ahead, off to the right, as if some large animal had appeared along the side of the road. Since deer were common in these parts, she slowed down, in case it decided to bolt across the road.

Holy smokes! That was no deer—it was a man! She slammed on her brakes as he dashed out from among the trees, right in front of her truck.

As she screeched to a stop, he just stood there, pinned in the full blaze of her headlights, holding his hands up, as if he was trying to flag her down. Gravel spun under her wheels, and everything loose on the front seat rocketed into the dashboard. Her heart was pounding and her whole body was singing with adrenaline, but it didn't interfere with her vision one bit.

"Dear God," she whispered.

Rowan McKenna. She should have known it would be him. Who else would rise up out of the trees, like some headless horseman in a bad dream? Who else would chase her all the way out here, collaring her just when she thought she was in the clear?

"Are you crazy?" she shouted at him, mostly for her own benefit, as she pounded the steering wheel. "You could've been run down like a jackrabbit!"

But he couldn't hear her. He was too busy standing there, peering at her through the blinding glare of her lights. The flash of white she'd seen was his pristine white shirt, glowing like a beacon through the darkness. He'd lost his dinner jacket and his black tie somewhere along the line, but his shirt was intact, sleeves rolled up, open at the neck, a little rumpled.

He was as knock-down, drag-out gorgeous as ever. Damn the man.

She felt like running him down while she still had a clear shot. All it would've taken was one wallop on the accelerator, and boom! He would've been flat as a pancake. No more Rowan. No more impossible, infuriating, meddlesome Rowan. It was tempting.

He shaded his eyes with one hand. "It's you," he said with evident relief, crossing to her side of the pickup.

He knows, she thought, and her pulse picked up even as her heart plummeted to the bottom of her stomach. Of course he'd recognized her immediately. How could he miss? After all, they'd spent the whole evening together, gazing at each other. He was a smart, perceptive man; he would have to see what was right before his eyes.

C.J. gripped the steering wheel so fiercely that her knuckles went white. What was she going to say? How could she explain?

Before she had a chance to think, he leaned in her window and demanded, "Have you seen a woman out here?"

She felt as if her wits had been tossed out the window a half mile back. Blankly she repeated, "A woman?"

"Yes, a woman." He was clearly impatient. "A beautiful woman. Like...like Cinderella."

"Cinderella?" she said weakly. His beautiful hair was tousled, but it gleamed black and soft in the faded moonlight. He looked hot and spent, as if he'd been running though the humid, sultry night. Running...after her.

C.J.'s heart took a little jump. He'd been running after her. It should've been as annoying as everything else about the man. So why was it so endearing? Why did she have the urge to beg his forgiveness and throw herself into his strong arms?

"I think she might be out here on the road," he said tersely. "Cinderella, er, that is, the woman I'm looking for, ran away from me at the country-club ball— the Firecracker Ball—and I think she must have come this way. I have to find her."

Reality descended upon her with a thud. He didn't recognize her.

The target of his frantic search was staring him right in the face, and he was clueless. C.J.'s hands twitched with the sudden need to slap his handsome face. So arrogant, so cocksure. And he didn't know her when he saw her. Some Prince Charming.

"Well?" he prompted. "Did you see her? You couldn't miss her. She was very tall and absolutely beautiful, like a model." He waved his hands in the air, indicating something like a human Barbie doll. If his hands were to be believed, his Cinderella was six feet tall, with more curves than a mountain road.

The fact that he was way off only made her more angry. C.J. was slim, not very curvaceous, and only five-six. Okay, so maybe she'd edged up to five-nine with those high heels, but still...

Oops. She suddenly realized that those very shoes were on the front seat, not three feet from Prince Charming. And with them should be a scattered set of fake fingernails, a white evening purse and one very distinctive white feathered mask.

Panicked, she sent a surreptitious glance in that direction. Luckily for her, all of the things she'd carelessly tossed on the seat had been dumped onto the floor when she'd slammed on the brakes. But they were still pretty obvious if he happened to look over there. Not to mention the wispy, frothy expanse of her stupid skirt, partially hidden by the steering wheel, but perfectly visible if he leaned any farther in her window.

Horror began to thread through her already frayed nerves. *I have to get out of here!*

"She was stunning. She looked like a princess," he went on dreamily, as C.J. nodded, trying to position herself to block his view and not to give in to hysteria. "Blond hair—curly and full. And violet eyes..."

Violet eyes? Oh, Lord! What would she screw up next? She still wore her contact lenses!

Thank goodness it was dark. Just to be on the safe side, she squinted at him and pulled the brim of her cap down a little farther over her still-violet eyes.

"I haven't seen anyone," she said abruptly, cutting off his besotted, completely inaccurate description of his fantasy woman. "Tell me, McKenna, did you have a lot to drink at this Firecracker thing you were at?"

"No," he said shortly. "Why?"

"Sounds to me like you're hallucinating." She managed a thin smile. "Beauty queens with violet eyes, running around on country roads in the middle of the night. Don't tell me—she had her pet pink elephant with her."

He stared at her, obviously surprised that she wasn't falling all over herself to help him in his ridiculous quest. "What are you talking about?"

"Maybe I have a firmer grip on reality than you do."

"I told you, I'm not drunk!"

"Yeah, well, I don't care if you are or not." She shook her head. "If you're telling the truth, and there really is a woman, then she probably ran away from you for a very good reason. Like maybe she thought you were an insufferable, arrogant jerk!"

As her words heated up, she began to realize just how angry she was. It was one thing to fool him for a whole night by pretending to be something that she wasn't, but it was quite another when he could look her straight in the eye and not even notice her. It made her want to hit him, right between the eyes.

"Either you've seen her or you haven't," he said coldly. "There's no reason to insult me."

"Pardon me if I don't like people popping up in front of my truck in the middle of nowhere," she shot back. "You scared the pants off me."

Except, of course, for the fact that she wasn't wearing any pants. All she had on was her white tutu. And if she didn't get away from him and his damn blue eyes within the next two minutes, she knew he'd see it for himself.

"What are you doing out here, anyway?" he asked, sounding suspicious all of a sudden. "Isn't it kind of late for a ride in the country?"

Oh, brother. At that moment, she couldn't have thought of a suitable story to save her life. "Look," she said quickly, starting to roll up her window, forcing him to back away or get his arm caught. "I haven't seen your runaway princess, and I can't sit around here all night. Take my advice—go back up to the club and party down with the Farleys and their pals. I'm sure that's a lot more fun than wandering around in the dark, just asking to get turned into roadkill."

"You can't just leave me here," he said darkly, but she planned to do just that. "At least give me a ride—"

But C.J. had had enough for one night. She put the truck in gear and pushed the accelerator, easing away from him.

"Wait!" he called out behind her, for the second time that night.

C.J. ignored it. As his image receded in her rear-view mirror, she hit the gas hard in her concentrated effort to be out of there. *Now*.

"LOOK, SOMEBODY in this town has *got* to know something." Rowan fixed his most lethal glare on Odell Watson, the town's one and only newspaper-man.

But Odell just grinned and flipped his thumbs against the edges of his suspenders. "I told you the last time you was in here, son. I never heard of any lady in Sparks like that one." He paused, clicking his tongue thoughtfully. "Did you try the Farley girls? They're the ones who do all the invitin'."

Rowan shuddered. "I wouldn't go near them," he said under his breath.

Odell's grin widened. "How 'bout Florette Bunch, over to the Five and Dime? Florette usually knows what's goin' on around town."

"Tried her," he returned shortly. He was trying to hold on to the raveled edges of his patience, but Lord knew it wasn't easy. "I also tried Bitty Delmar at Petticoat Junction, who said she didn't sell a dress like that, and Lurlene at the beauty shop, who swears she didn't do her hair."

"Vesta Smalls?"

"Yes."

"Geneva Lugden?"

"Yes," he said between gritted teeth, remembering the sticky-sweet cookies and bilge-water coffee he'd endured as he cut a swath through Sparks's finer citizens' living rooms in his futile search for information. He now knew more than he'd ever wanted to about the ins and outs of this small town's life, and he'd even agreed to judge their local beauty contest in a weak moment.

But he still knew not one damn thing about the Cinderella he was seeking.

"Came up empty, huh?"

"Stone-cold empty." He raked a hand through the dark strands of his hair as he paced in front of Odell's desk. "I've talked to everybody I can think of, everybody I can remember being at the ball. But nobody knows anything. And I just don't buy it. A woman does not appear out of nowhere and then just vanish, without somebody knowing *something*."

"Sounds like this one did," Odell remarked cheerfully.

With his hand in his pocket, once more brushing against his souvenir from the Firecracker Ball, Rowan muttered, "And all I have left to show for the evening is half a bottle rocket."

"Would've thought somebody would've known the girl," Odell said thoughtfully.

Darkly Rowan remarked, "Unless they're all conspiring to keep me away from her."

"Now why would we do that?"

It was a crazy idea, and he knew it. But none of this made sense. He tried to explain. "Ever since I got here, Sparks has been buzzing with the idea that I'm going to take over the fireworks factory." He paused, narrowing his gaze at Odell. "Maybe the people in this town are loyal to Buzz."

"What's that got to do with your missing lady friend?"

"Buzz had the idea that I might be persuaded to link up—" he grimaced, but kept going "—with one of his daughters, to forestall a buyout. Trust me when I say that's never going to happen."

"Never seemed very likely to me," Odell said with a grin.

"I don't know—the whole idea is nuts. But how else . . . ?" He shook his head. "I've got to find her. That's the only answer. Once I find her, it won't matter why we've been kept apart."

This time Odell gave him a look that smacked of sympathy. "So what can I do to help, son?"

"Buzz said you had a copy of the guest list," Rowan explained. "He said they'd sent you one to print in the social pages."

"Well, let me think a minute." The old man chewed his lower lip, popped his suspenders back and forth and stared into space. "I reckon they sent me something or other like that a couple of weeks ago. And I reckon I threw it out."

"You threw it out?" In a few more minutes, Rowan felt sure he would vault over the desk and strangle old Odell with his own suspenders. "So you don't have the list?"

Odell shook his head sadly.

"And you don't know anybody who fits the description?"

"Run it by me again."

"Tall, blond, beautiful. She was wearing a white dress. Let me tell you, Odell," Rowan said with a sardonic smile, "if you saw this woman, you'd know who I was talking about."

Once again, the editor of the Sparks *Sentinel* shook his head. "Rings no bells, son. Rings no bells."

"Dammit." He was running out of options. "Who can she be?"

Rowan scowled. He'd already canvassed the whole town, and the story was the same everywhere: they all wanted to know whether he was going to buy the fireworks factory, and nobody knew a damn thing about the woman in white.

In the end, he'd talked to everybody. Everybody except C. J. Bede, that is. After she'd practically run him down in her haste to be unfriendly and uncooperative, he didn't think it was wise to go and ask for her help again. Besides, she hadn't been at the ball, so what could she tell him?

He frowned. C.J. was still a puzzle. He honestly couldn't figure her out, or figure out why *he* cared that she so obviously didn't like him. But the fact was, her animosity got under his skin. It rankled.

He simply wasn't used to people who hated him on sight. "Well, I don't think she hates me," he mumbled.

"Who?" Odell asked brightly.

"C.J." Rowan shrugged. "She seems to have taken an instant dislike to me."

"I thought you were worried about your woman in white. What's C.J. got to do with it?"

"Nothing," he said hastily. "It's just that..."

Even he didn't know where his thoughts were going this time, or why C.J. kept popping into his head. Certainly he was much more interested in the whereabouts of his mystery woman than he was in the reason for C.J.'s prickly attitude.

But her behavior had surprised him enough that he'd found himself asking questions about her, too, as he made his way around town. Trust the good citizens of Sparks to dismiss her as easily as they dismissed his search for Cinderella.

"None of us have ever been able to figure out that girl," confided smug Bitty Delmar, who owned the Petticoat Junction dress shop. "No better than she should be, that one."

Geneva Lugden had been less oblique. "Too big for her britches. Thinks she's smarter than the rest of us."

Whereas Buzz Farley had gotten redder in the face than usual and simply refused to discuss C.J. at all.

Rowan couldn't help but be intrigued. What had C.J. ever done to them? Or perhaps more likely, what had they done to her?

In some ways, she was more worthy of his interest than the enigmatic Cinderella from the ball. After all, at least C.J. was real. She was also smart and blunt and feisty. She had no qualms about standing up to him, and he could count on the fingers of one hand the people who were willing to do that.

A part of him—a very small part, to be sure—wondered whether his desperate approach to this search was simply an attempt to prove to C.J. that he wasn't a nut case. After all, it still irritated him that she hadn't believed his story. She'd even had the gall to suggest he was drunk, or out of his mind. Maybe his competitive urges had snapped into gear, and he was only trying to mark up a victory in the continuing battle to get C.J. to take him seriously.

"Dammit, that's not it," he swore under his breath.

"What's not what?"

Forget C.J., he ordered himself. The woman in white came first.

"Odell," he said abruptly. "You sure you don't have anything on the Firecracker Ball? Anything Buzz or his family might have sent you?"

"Nothing from before the ball, if that's what you mean," Odell said again. "But I do have an article about it, ready to go in next week's paper, plus the pictures Chatty Smalls, my social reporter, took at the Ball. Would that help?"

"Your social reporter?" What in God's name was the *Sentinel,* circulation 800, doing with a social reporter? But Rowan's curiosity was aroused, against his better judgment. "Did you say she took pictures of the guests?"

"Uh-huh."

He had never considered the idea that a photo of his mystery woman might exist. His whole body went on alert. "All of them? All of the guests?"

"I don't know. I pulled out one of Buzz and Mim Farley to go with the article, but I haven't looked at the rest. You want 'em?"

Did he want them? Once again, he had the urge to leap over the desk and get things moving a bit more quickly. But with his first real break staring him in the face, he couldn't blow it. Instead, he clenched his hands into fists and said evenly, "Yes, I would like that very much."

The editor rustled around on his desk for a few long moments, mumbling to himself, finally saying, "Well, they're not here. Let me go look in the back."

As Rowan cooled his heels there in the main office, growing increasingly impatient, he heard the noise of shuffling papers and Odell's tuneless whistle back in the bowels of the newspaper office. Ready to jump out of his skin, he jammed a hand into his pocket and rubbed his thumb up and down that damn bottle rocket.

He had to find her. He had to.

But right now, his only chance hinged on an old coot of a newspaperman locating a photograph taken by someone named Chatty. It wasn't a comforting thought.

"Here we go!" Odell announced, wandering back into the room. He slapped a stack of black-and-white photos into Rowan's waiting hands, and then waved a few typed sheets of paper. "And it's the dangedest thing. I found that list you were looking for, too. The guest list. It was paperclipped to Chatty's article. Isn't that funny?"

"Great, great," Rowan murmured as he quickly riffled through a stack of black-and-white pictures of fireworks. Who took photographs of fireworks in black and white? They all looked alike. Finally, he got to pictures of people. Unfortunately most of them were out of focus and poorly lit, and quite a few cut their subjects' heads off.

But then he found it.

He was plowing through an endless series of prints of the ballroom, when suddenly he saw himself. There he was, off to the side of a wide shot of the whole dance floor. Karla Farley and her hideous mermaid dress were posing front and center, but way back in the corner, Rowan saw his own profile. Staring past him, looking right into the camera, was the woman in white.

His hand trembled, shaking the picture enough that he had to steady himself to see. He couldn't believe he had finally found incontrovertible evidence that she really existed.

They were dancing. He pressed his eyes closed, remembering what it had felt like to hold her like that. Suddenly memories of that night overpowered him. He could hear the music, he could smell her perfume and he could feel her slender body in his arms—

"Hey," Odell interrupted, and the images vanished. "This is about her. Chatty's story—she wrote, 'Local lovelies had their noses put out of joint when celebrity visitor Rowan McKenna occupied himself with someone else all evening, someone the ball organizers swear was not on the invite list. Who was she? The Misses Farley say it was a party crasher, not from around here, perhaps come to steal wealthy guests' jewelry, but thwarted when McKenna tried to rip her mask off and she had to flee.'"

"What a bunch of nonsense," Rowan muttered.

Odell kept reading. "'I don't know who she was,' Karla Farley told this reporter, 'but she better never show her face around here again.'" He smiled. "That's a darn good story. I may have to hire Chatty full-time."

Rowan held up the picture, desperate for an answer. "Tell me, Odell, once and for all. Do you know her?"

The old man tipped his head to one side, taking his infernal time as he considered the photo. "You know, that picture's pretty fuzzy, and she's got that mask thing covering half her face, so I can't say for sure." He paused, started to speak, and then paused again.

Finally he said, "There is something very familiar about that girl."

Behind him, Rowan heard the front door slide open slowly. He turned.

Looking as skittish as ever, C. J. Bede walked in the door.

Chapter Six

"Almost had it there for a minute," Odell said, frowning down at a picture lying on the counter. "But it's gone now."

Meanwhile, Rowan gave her the same intense scrutiny he always did. "What are you looking at?" C.J. asked warily.

But Odell answered. "This darn picture of Mr. McKenna's." He shook his head sadly. "I can't seem to get a fix on whatever it was I thought I saw. I reckon I was mistaken."

Rowan turned to the old man. "Come on, Odell, if there's even a hint, I need to know."

"Nope," he said. "Sorry, son."

Automatically, C.J. pulled her baseball cap farther down over her eyes, glancing from one face to the other. What were they talking about, and why did she feel so sure it had something to do with her?

It was really a very stupid move to be here. But she'd been so anxious to hear the bad news, she'd felt she *had* to come by.

News had to be out by now that Rowan McKenna was interested in Farley Fireworks, and the stock would be going up fast. It was only a matter of time, and it was going to destroy all of her well-laid plans.

Unless, of course, the Cinderella scheme had mixed him up so badly that he had forgotten about the factory. If he showed no interest in fireworks, maybe the stock would fall as swiftly as it had climbed. It was what she was hoping for, but looking at the man in all his masculine, overwhelming, interfering glory, it seemed small comfort.

"I'll come back later," she murmured, backing toward the door.

"Oh, no, you stay right there," Rowan said darkly. "I want to talk to you."

"To me?" She kept backing up. "Why?"

He took her hand, pulling her toward him, and she immediately felt a jolt of electricity pass from his warm fingers to her wrist. Did he feel it, too? Was their undeniable chemistry going to be her undoing?

A look of utter surprise flashed across Rowan's face before he abruptly dropped her hand. "I, uh, have something to show you," he muttered, reaching for the photograph Odell had been examining when she came in.

"What is it?"

"Proof," he said triumphantly. "I told you she was real."

C.J. immediately stiffened. "Who?"

"The girl. *My* girl. The one I was looking for after the country-club ball, when I saw you on the road. My Cinderella. Don't you remember?"

How could she possibly forget? "Are you still harping on that crazy story?" she asked. "I thought you'd give up on it after a good night's sleep."

"It's not a crazy story." He slapped the photo down on the counter in front of her. More softly he added, "And believe me, I haven't had a good night's sleep since I met her."

Neither have I. Gazing into Rowan McKenna's hopeful, miserable blue eyes, C.J. felt a definite pang in the area of her heart.

She tore her gaze away and stared down at the counter.

"So, what do you think?" he demanded. "Do you recognize her?"

For the first time, she took a good look at the picture he was waving in front of her. It was partially out of focus, and clearly the work of an amateur, but even that couldn't keep her from identifying the scene or the people. Her heart took a little leap, and she had to remind herself to keep breathing.

Good God! There she was. She hadn't been aware there was a photographer at the ball.

Well, that was hardly surprising. She hadn't been aware of anything but Rowan and the music...and the heady feeling, for the first time in her life, that she was the most desirable woman in the room.

She felt as if she was going to faint. She felt as if she was going to blurt out the whole thing.

Not that he'd believe her if she did. After all, he'd had ample opportunities to realize that Cinderella was merely C.J. in disguise. But when he looked at C.J., he obviously didn't see the princess he was so enamored of. In fact, he probably didn't see anything he liked at all.

"I think I'm the wrong person to ask about what goes on at the country club," she said coolly. And she shoved the photo back at him, thanking her lucky stars that the photographer had done such a lousy job. "Odell, do you have those stock quotes?"

But the wily old newspaperman had conveniently disappeared for the moment.

"I thought you might know who she was." McKenna set his jaw firmly as he regarded her for a long moment. "You're the one person I've met in this town who I thought might tell me the truth."

That was rich. At the moment, she wasn't sure she'd recognize the truth if it jumped up and bit her. She edged away from him. "I can't help you, Mr. McKenna."

"So we're back to Mr. McKenna again, are we?"

Her gaze fixed on his handsome face before she could stop it. God, he was gorgeous. She could look at him all day.

Those crystal blue eyes, with their dark, spiky lashes, were so inviting, so knowing. And then there was his perfect nose, not aquiline or snippy, just perfect. He had narrow, mocking lips, although the bottom one was a shade fuller than the top one, reminding her of the passion he could unleash when he had a mind to.

She couldn't help but remember what it had been like when he'd kissed her under the stars, when those lips had trailed along her bare shoulder... She shivered at the memory.

Heavenly as it was, that one kiss hadn't been nearly enough. She felt a deep ache of disappointment, knowing that she would never taste his mouth on hers again.

Oh, Clementine, she thought despairingly. *What* are you doing to yourself?

Time to look below the collar, to get away from his lips before she lost her mind. He was dressed casually today. It didn't make a particle of difference. He was devastating no matter what he wore.

Today, he had on a white button-down shirt, open at the neck, revealing his smooth, tanned neck, making her want to pop off all the rest of those irritating little buttons and expose his chest and his shoulders to her hungry eyes.

He looked good enough to ravish. Right then, right there in the newspaper office, with Odell Watson watching, if it came to that.

Stop it, she commanded herself. Sternly she took herself and her wayward emotions in hand, purposely turning away from him until she had better control.

As far as her revenge plans were concerned, she had to remember that he was the enemy. Just by coming to town, he had screwed up everything.

Behind her, he said, "I didn't think you were in league with the rest of them."

"In league? With the rest of who?"

"This town." Clenching his jaw, he announced, "Buzz and his daughters have a vested interest in my not finding this woman. I'm not sure if he wants to snare me for his daughters to keep the factory in the family, or just for my bank account, but they're definitely not happy there's an interloper."

If anybody had a vested interest in Rowan's not finding his mystery woman, it was Clementine Jemima Bede. She could hardly tell him that, however. C.J. digested the rest of his information. So he knew the sisters Farley were after him. Well, that was no surprise. He might not be able to recognize Cinderella once she was out of her ball gown, but at least he knew an ugly stepsister when he saw one.

He continued, "I get the idea you don't like the Farleys much. I haven't figured out exactly why, but I can tell there's a story there somewhere."

C.J. had to hide a gulp. Had she been that obvious? She racked her brain for what she'd said, how she'd given herself away.

It was an important part of her master plan that she remain completely hidden. No one must guess who was behind Buzz's problems—not until the last minute when, with her revenge complete, Clementine could make her grand entrance and throw Buzz's failures in his face.

Take that, you cad! You destroyed my mother, and now I've destroyed you. How does it feel, Mr. Bigshot?

But she'd never told anyone that—not her mother, not Miss Pru . . . not even Samantha, her cat. So how did Rowan know she hated the Farley clan?

He gave her a speculative glance. "I keep thinking about that sampler on the wall at your office, about rage and fury and women scorned."

There was a long pause. "And what does that have to do with the Farleys?" she asked quietly, carefully.

"I don't know." He smiled wickedly. "Yet."

She began to tap two fingers on the counter in a staccato rhythm. "One way or the other, it's none of your business."

"Let's just say I've made it my business."

Rowan eased over until he was lounging against the counter. Reaching out, he put his hand over hers, stilling her fingers. Once again, her skin tingled and her nerve endings sizzled the moment he touched her. Looking up into his eyes, she knew he felt it, too.

His voice was soft and sexy when he said, "You intrigue me, Clementine. You and your bad attitude and your sassy little sampler. I can't quite figure out how you fit into the picture of this town. And when something—or someone—intrigues me, I don't rest until I've solved the mystery."

"I guess that's why you're all fired up to find that Cinderella of yours." She pulled her hand out from under his and jammed it into her jeans pocket. Angrily she added, "She's not even a real woman to you, is she? Just a mystery that you want solved."

"You sound like that bothers you," he mused. "Why do you care how I feel about *her?*"

C.J. turned away. "It just makes me mad, that's all. Tearing up the town, going crazy, and yet, once you find her, you'll probably throw her back, like some lousy catfish that was an inch too small."

She'd thought she could sting him with her words. But he surprised her by agreeing.

"That could very well happen." He smiled, giving her a sardonic grin that barely hinted at a dimple. "I have very high standards."

"High standards? Ha!" She looked him right in the eye. "You're nothing but a two-bit pirate. If you see something you think you might, maybe *conceivably* want, as long as it's ripe and ready, you climb on board and plunder away."

He leaned closer. "Are you ripe and ready, Clementine?"

She refused to be deterred, and she continued on the offensive. "Aren't you even going to defend yourself? Or are you proud of the fact that you're no better than a common thief? You steal your prizes, you use them up and then you throw them away. And that's what you have in mind for your poor Cinderella, isn't it?"

His jaw clenched. "I don't steal. What I get, I take fair and square."

"Not fair. Not square."

"I do what I have to."

C.J. raised her chin. "So do I. And if that includes taking you down a few pegs, so be it."

That took him aback. She wasn't sure if it was simply her willingness to fight back, or maybe the fact that her verbal volleys had hit a sore spot, but she saw surprise sparkle in his beautiful eyes. He murmured, "Is that a threat, Clementine?"

"Just a warning."

Rowan smiled lazily. "I have to remember not to underestimate you. You could be a formidable enemy if you wanted to."

She took it as a compliment. And she loved it.

If he hadn't been so gorgeous, if he hadn't been standing smack-dab in the middle of her plans like one fabulous-looking roadblock, she'd have been tempted to grab him and kiss him, as herself, as C. J. Bede, just to see what happened.

"I don't know, Clementine," he said, watching her carefully. "You strike me as honest to the core. If you really did know the woman in this photo, I think you'd tell me the truth, if for no other reason than you don't know any other way to behave."

Oh, brother. When was he going to give up on this honesty stuff and stop making her feel like a criminal? "I told you not to call me Clementine."

His smile widened. "I know."

"Ahem," Odell said loudly. "When are you two going to stop chitchatting and get out of my office? In case nobody noticed, I've got a newspaper to run here."

"Oh, that's right." Rowan turned, swiftly abandoning his scuffle with C.J., tapping the photograph where it sat on the counter. "Do you have the negative for this, Odell?"

C.J. came back to earth in one fell swoop. He might enjoy slinging insults with her, but in Rowan's eyes, she'd always rate below his insufferable Cinderella fantasy.

"I'd like to blow it up," he continued. "To get a better look at her. Then maybe I'll run it in the paper. You know, in a box, with a caption like 'Who is the Woman in White?'"

Odell's ears perked up as C.J.'s heart stood still. The old man cheerfully demanded, "You talking about taking out an ad? Run every day? A full page?"

Rowan nodded, getting a gleam in his eye that she didn't like one bit. "And not just here—in all the papers, from Milwaukee to Madison and Green Bay. I'll offer a reward. That ought to make somebody come forward."

"Don't you think you're getting a bit carried away?"

She was frantically trying to think if there was anyone in the state of Wisconsin who might recognize her. The photo was pretty bad, but was it bad enough? Would her mother know who it was? Would Miss Pru spill the beans for a reward?

Or was there some way to stave this off? Maybe she could break into the office after-hours and steal the negative.

Good Lord! Who'd ever thought McKenna would take things this far?

"You just admitted she means nothing to you," she tried. "Why go to all this trouble?"

"I said it might turn out that I don't want to keep her," he amended. "But I won't know until I find her, will I? And then I'll decide."

The arrogant, insufferable swine. He wanted to hunt down this nonexistent woman, not because he'd fallen in love that starlit night, not even because he wanted to see her again, but just to give himself back the upper hand!

"What if this woman has a reason she doesn't want to be found?" she asked quickly. "Are you ready to wreck her life if she has a husband stashed somewhere?"

"Or maybe she's an escapee from prison," Odell added hopefully.

But Rowan only shook his head firmly. "I've got to find her. Whatever it takes. I'll turn this state upside down if I have to."

Even though she questioned his motives, C.J. believed he was serious. Suddenly her life promised to be a living hell. How could she fix something *this* bad?

"Get me that negative," Rowan told Odell. "I want her in tomorrow's paper. Got that?"

Tomorrow's paper? But there was no time to prepare, no time to plan a counterstrategy!

All Odell said was "Yessir."

And with an abrupt nod for C.J., Rowan swept out of the office before she could make any more protests. "This is ridiculous!" she exclaimed, shouting at poor, innocent Odell. "You can't do this."

"I sure can." The old man smiled gleefully. "Like takin' candy from a baby. Did you get a good look at that thing? It's only gonna get blurrier when he blows it up. Ain't nobody gonna recognize nothin' from that picture. Why, he could be runnin' it for months. But he'll be payin' me every day, just the same."

"Right," she said faintly. She only hoped Odell knew what he was talking about when it came to photographs. Otherwise her goose was cooked.

"So, you still want those stock quotes?" He rooted around on his desk for a long minute. "Chatty took 'em off the computer first thing this morning. That girl's comin' in handy. I have more trouble with that darn machine." Finally he held up a sheaf of computer-generated sheets and marched over to the counter to dangle them in front of C.J. "If it's Farley stock you're looking at, it's jumping."

"No, that's not it," she managed, pretending to zero in on IBM and GM, but it sounded weak even to her own ears. No wonder everyone in town knew she didn't like the Farleys. Here she was, hanging over their stock prices like a vulture, hoping for bad news.

"Coulda guessed it'd be going up, what with that Prince of Takeovers in town."

"Mmm-hmm," she said vaguely, giving the mutual funds the once-over.

"But now that Mr. McKenna's all caught up in locating this mystery woman of his, and paying no attention to Fireworks, I expect the Farley stock will be dropping like a rock." Odell tipped his head to one side. "That what you think, C.J.?

He had put his ink-stained fingers on the very nub of her plan to divert Rowan. She hadn't done a darn thing with interrogation yet, but intrigue and elude were going gangbusters. In fact, he was so hot to find his Cinderella that he had forgotten the firecracker factory even existed.

It was exactly what she'd been hoping for way back when, when she'd hatched this idiotic part of her revenge scheme. He now appeared to be so bamboozled by the mysterious woman at the ball that he was voluntarily walking off the takeover playing field.

She had what she wanted. So why was she so miserable? Was it because her face, blurry though it was, was about to be plastered all over the state of Wisconsin?

Or maybe because she'd had the best time in her entire life that night at the ball, and she could never, ever repeat the performance.

"Too bad the boom in Farley stock isn't gonna last," Odell remarked, flipping at his suspenders with the pads of his thumbs. "You look like that news has downright depressed you, C.J."

"What? Oh, sure."

She was depressed, all right. But the rise and fall in Fireworks stock didn't have a darned thing to do with it.

"Miss Pru, are you ready yet?"

C.J. was feeling fidgety. She had spent all morning making blueberry muffins at Miss Pru's house, and she had volunteered to drive her elderly neighbor to the town's annual Fourth of July picnic. It was one of three functions Miss Pru attended every year, just like clockwork.

The Christmas pageant and the Labor Day Founders' parade made a certain amount of sense, especially since Miss Pru was the last of the Hopmillers, and as such, she had the duty of handing out the two Hopmiller Prizes, awarded for the best Christmas decorations and the best float in the parade. Every year, Miss Pru did herself up as grandly as possible, including white gloves and high lace collars, to present "her" September and December awards.

But C.J. had never understood the reason behind attending the Independence Day picnic. Standing outside in the July heat and humidity just to watch the town stuff itself with deviled eggs and Florette Bunch's strawberry-rhubarb pie was not her idea of a good time.

This year it was going to be even worse. Rowan McKenna was going to be there. She was going to be forced to look at his dad-blasted smug face again and pretend she wasn't the woman of his dreams.

"I'm not the woman of his dreams," C.J. whispered. "*She* is—that stupid woman in white. And that's not me."

She cut off her melancholy thoughts just as her diminutive friend descended the staircase. Miss Prudence was wearing an ice blue lace dress that wouldn't have looked out of place at a tea party for Teddy

Roosevelt. In honor of the occasion, she'd pinned a red-and-white-and-blue cockade to her bodice and added a red hatband to her navy blue hat.

"You look lovely," C.J. assured her friend.

"Thank you, my dear," the old lady said sweetly. "Although I'm sure your attire is more the thing these days."

C.J. suddenly wished she had gone for something a little spiffier. But white jeans with a ruffled chambray shirt *was* dressed up for her, especially since she was wearing a brand-new, bright red baseball cap, with her ponytail poked out the space in the back.

"Are we late?" Miss Pru asked as C.J. shepherded her and two huge baskets of blueberry muffins out the door. "You seem in a bit of a rush."

She held open the passenger door to Miss Pru's large and largely undriven Buick. "I'm sorry. I don't know what's gotten into me. I'm just feeling anxious today."

"Hmm." Her elderly friend regarded her with inquisitive gray eyes. "Will we be seeing that interesting McKenna boy at today's festivities?"

"I suppose so." C.J. made a point of concentrating on starting the car and pulling it slowly down the driveway.

Miss Pru patted the basket she'd tucked neatly on her knees as she remarked innocently, "I'm very anxious to meet him. He looked so very attractive when I saw him in my spyglass, and I would have loved seeing him at the ball. So dashing! I'm certain you made a lovely couple—"

"Don't our muffins smell good?" C.J. interrupted. She chattered on about food and decorations and anything else she could think of to keep from wandering back to *him,* until finally they were parked near the picnic grounds.

There were big bunches of red and blue balloons, and a banner stretched between the gates to the park that read Happy July Fourth! as it prominently featured cascading fireworks of the Farley variety. Picnic tables covered with red-and-white checkered tablecloths had been pulled into a U-shape, and local cooks were busy setting up their fried chicken and three-bean salads.

"Isn't that your mother?" Miss Pru asked brightly, as they slowly crossed the grass. "Ivy is such a sweet girl."

C.J.'s mother was hardly a girl anymore, but compared to Miss Pru, practically anyone would be a spring chicken.

"And who's that Ivy is talking to?" the old lady continued. "Why, I believe it's the McKenna boy. Now isn't that a stroke of luck, since I did so want to meet your beau."

"He's not my beau," she said quickly, but her mind was racing.

Rowan McKenna, talking to her mother? C.J. had to resist the impulse to break into a run. Or maybe a cold sweat.

C.J. tried to look on the bright side, to be glad that what was probably only a casual conversation for him would do a world of good for her mom. Since Ivy Bede was the town's favorite fallen woman, who had never even attempted to provide a father for her child, there was a certain faction in Sparks who made a point of publicly snubbing her. But now, if they saw her getting to be pals with their rich and powerful visitor, the town battleaxes would have to unbend and be a little nicer. Wouldn't they?

"Clemmy! Clemmy!" Ivy Bede hailed, waving her arms. "Over here, honey."

C.J. didn't know which was more dangerous— joining them and hearing what they were talking about, or avoiding them and having to wonder. Dutifully, with Miss Pru and her baskets in tow, she walked up to the part of the pavilion where they stood. Her mother made quick work of the introductions, and then launched into her usual fussing about C.J.'s appearance.

"Clemmy, honey, why do you always wear those ugly hats?" she fretted, poking at the brim of C.J.'s red cap.

"I sunburn easily, Mom," she said for what must have been the ninety-fifth time, but she kept her voice light, and her hat firmly in place. "You know I always have to cover up."

Rowan lifted one eyebrow. "I keep wondering what you're hiding under there. But you know, C.J., I'm sort of getting used to you and your hats." He tweaked her bill. "This one's kind of cute."

As her mother giggled, C.J. decided she wasn't going to ponder the implications of that statement. Meanwhile, Ivy exclaimed, "Sweetie, Rowan and I have had the nicest chat. He's been telling me that he wants you to make him a barn! Isn't that wonderful news?" She smiled eagerly. "Another job for you, hon."

C.J. still couldn't imagine *him* living in a barn. "You aren't really serious, are you?"

"Of course he is," her mother assured her, as Rowan gave her that lazy grin that made her stomach do flip-flops. "And he's also been telling me the most amazing story. Clemmy, honey, you won't believe it. He met a real Cinderella at the ball. Who would ever think this could happen in our little town?"

"I would," Miss Pru said brightly.

Ivy smiled mistily. "But then she just vanished into thin air. Ever since, dear Rowan has been trying desperately to find his Cinderella. Oh, it's enough to break your heart."

"So you haven't found her yet?" C.J. asked sweetly. "Too bad."

Rowan gave her a dark look. He looked downright surly, and she knew she was risking a nasty bout of temper, but she went on, "I saw the picture in the paper. What a shame it turned out so fuzzy."

"Oh, yes, I saw that, too," Ivy put in.

C.J. glanced over with alarm. She'd known the chances were good that her mom, along with everybody else in town, would see the picture in the paper. But C.J. had also felt reasonably certain that not even her own mother would know she was the one. An already indistinct photo, poorly reproduced, of a white mask against a pale face and blond hair had turned out to be mostly just white space. Thank goodness.

But of all the people in the world...

"'Who is the Woman in White?'" Ivy continued, blissfully unaware her daughter was about to expire from nerves. "I wish I knew her so I could help you out, you poor thing. It's so romantic."

C.J. allowed herself a short moment of relief, as Miss Pru protested, "What picture? I didn't see any picture!"

"We'll get you a copy," Rowan interjected. "Who knows, Miss Hopmiller, you might be the one person who can identify her."

The old lady's eyes were definitely twinkling when she said, "I might, indeed."

"You won't identify anything from *that*," C.J. said with what she hoped was conviction. She was praying her friend would stop dropping hints and start showing a little discretion, but she was afraid a judicious elbow would injure her old bones.

"It's a shame there was only that one picture," Ivy said, clicking her tongue.

"Don't worry." Rowan took Ivy's hand and patted it, smiling kindly as he said, "I've got another idea."

C.J. couldn't miss how sweet he was being to her mother, but she still felt a little apprehensive about him and his ideas.

"I talked to a police sketch artist from Milwaukee," he said. "I'm going to send out flyers. Lots and lots of flyers. There'll be one on every tree in Wisconsin."

"What?" C.J. squeaked, as a loud "Hmmph" sounded from behind her mother, followed by "What's the meaning of this?"

Momentarily forgetting the flyer fiasco, their little group turned to see what the interruption was all about.

"Some people!" Mim Farley, the matriarch of the clan, said loudly. She was decked out in red-and-white flounces, and her sturdy form resembled nothing so much as a battleship. "Really, Rowan, hasn't anyone warned you? If you want to get on with Sparks society, it's not a good idea to consort with *this* sort of person."

"I'm afraid these lovely ladies are far more likely to be tarnished by the association than I am," he said gallantly, squeezing Ivy's hand as he smiled with reassurance. But his words were wasted on the odious Mrs. Farley. C.J. watched as her own mother's expression wilted, and Mim and her wobbly chins geared themselves for another salvo.

Time to take action. "Excuse me," C.J. announced. "We were just leaving."

Collecting her mother on one side, and Miss Pru and the blueberry muffins on the other, C.J. made a beeline for the food tables, ignoring Rowan's surprised gaze. She didn't care where she was headed, but she knew she had to get away before Mim started using words like "tramp" and "wanton" and Ivy burst into tears.

Leaving Rowan in Mim's control was not a pleasant prospect, and C.J. tried not to get any more anxious than she already was, what with Miss Pru's loose lips and the idea of that darned picture floating around.

But this new wrinkle could be the worst yet. Rowan was already curious enough about the antipathy between her and the Farleys. And now Mim was back there, giving him an earful.

What exactly would the old bat tell him?

She hazarded a glance back over her shoulder. Poor Rowan. Mim was practically glued to him, her mouth going a mile a minute, as he gazed over her head, staring right at C.J. "Help," he mouthed silently.

C.J. sighed. Once she got her mother and Miss Pru safely out of the line of fire, she knew what she had to do. She had to go back and rescue Rowan from the clutches of Mim Farley. She was just that kind of woman.

Chapter Seven

Thank God C.J. came back for him. He'd tried every excuse he could think of, and Mim hadn't even stopped for breath. Short of knocking her down and making a run for it, he was stuck. He might be ruthless and hard-hearted, but even Rowan McKenna was too polite to knock down a woman just because her conversation was tedious.

But then C.J. marched up, removed Mim's hand from his arm, neatly inserted herself in between and announced loudly, "Excuse me, Mim, but Rowan and I have business to discuss."

While Mrs. Farley stood there quivering with indignation, Rowan took his opportunity, grabbing C.J.'s hand and hightailing it out of there.

"This way," she whispered, leading him back around the pavilion and into a more secluded, tree-shaded area of the park. "I think we're safe back here."

He made sure no one was following, and then sank down against the trunk of a big oak tree with a sigh of relief. "I owe you big time for that one," he said, reaching up to pull her down onto the grass next to him. "God, those Farleys are impossible."

She gave him a small smile. "I know."

He'd never noticed how captivating her smile was. Or maybe he'd never caught it before, hidden as it was in the shadow of her ever-present baseball cap. But with her head tipped back, he had the chance to really appreciate it. Her smile wasn't polished or practiced, but it had a hint of freshness and mischief he found very appealing.

"Finally we agree on something," he teased, keeping an eye on that smile he liked so much. "You know, Clementine, you're very pretty when you're being agreeable." And he was pleased to see pink color brighten her cheeks. "Why, Clementine, you're blushing. Are you embarrassed that someone appreciates you?"

"I think you're trying to butter me up to stay on my good side," she said shrewdly.

"Well, there is that." He edged closer, leaning in to tap one finger against the tip of her impudent little nose. "But you're still very pretty."

Her blush deepened, and she batted his hand away. "You don't have to get all gooey just because I saved you from Mim, you know. I wouldn't let my worst enemy suffer that kind of torture."

He laughed, enjoying her irreverence. "Does that mean I'm not your worst enemy?"

"Not by a long shot," she said quietly.

There was a different tone to her words, something a bit more serious, that told him he should be very glad *not* to be on her enemies' list. He would've been very interested to find out who was, however. Rowan watched her, trying to figure out what was going on under that guarded expression. She was a very curious, mercurial woman, and he found himself wondering, once again, what secrets she was hiding.

"Well, thanks, anyway," he said lightly. "After all, you even stooped to lying on my behalf."

"It wasn't lying. We do have business to discuss." C.J. pulled up her knees, crossing her arms around them. She had long, slim legs, and they looked great in those white jeans of hers. Why hadn't he noticed how well she was put together before? C.J. was just full of surprises. "That is," she continued, pulling his attention away from her legs and back to her words, "if you were serious when you said you wanted one of my barns."

"Absolutely." Rowan grinned, feeling suddenly triumphant. Yes, he did want one of her barns. He couldn't imagine anything better. Actually, looking at her pretty little mouth, he could imagine several... "What changed your mind?"

"Believe it or not, it's that you were nice to my mother." She blushed again. "I suppose that sounds silly, but my mother is important to me," she said awkwardly. "The way you talked to her back there, and stood up for her when Mim said she wasn't good enough... It was very nice. Thank you."

"It was nothing," he told her, and he meant it. He was astonished that all of his best attempts at charm had fallen flat with C.J., but then one innocent little conversation impressed her. "I liked your mother. I thought she was very sweet." He smiled ruefully. "I like mothers in general, I guess. Mine's a lot tougher than yours, but I'm pretty fond of her, too."

It was her turn to look astonished. "I never thought of you with a mother."

"Everybody's got one. Even me." He stretched out his legs, encroaching on her space, enjoying the idea that he'd thrown C.J. a curve. "In fact, my mother was the reason I asked you about a barn in the first place. I thought I'd buy it for her."

"Oh. Not for you."

She seemed disappointed, but he was bound and determined not to screw up this newfound peace accord. "For me, too," he said quickly. "But it's hard to find gifts my mother will accept. Your barns seemed special enough that I thought she might go for it."

"Special?"

"Very special. There was one in particular I really liked." He frowned, trying to remember which picture on her office wall had caught his eye. "It was behind your desk, next to the sampler, an interior view of a big, open room. I think it had a quilt on one wall, a big fireplace, and a red sofa with a cat sitting on it."

"That's *my* house," she said suddenly. "Where I live. That's the one you like?"

He nodded, enjoying the spark of pleasure that lit up the depths of her golden hazel eyes. Had he ever seen what color they were? He didn't think so, but for some reason, that warm shade of honey brown surprised him.

Why did he expect her eyes to be blue? Or maybe violet?

Cinderella, of course. Dammit, anyway. He was imagining his dream woman everywhere now, even going so far as to cast her in C.J.'s place, interrupting a very nice moment with a perfectly lovely woman.

"What's the matter?" C.J. asked abruptly.

"It's nothing." But the mood was destroyed. "Look, I'm sorry. I just looked at your eyes, and I noticed what color they were."

She sat back, self-conscious, and dipped her head so that her cap cast her face in shadow. "They're just a normal color. They're just brown."

"Actually, they're a beautiful color, and they're hazel, not brown. Believe me, there's nothing wrong with your eyes." His hasty, clumsy remarks were making things worse, and he could've kicked himself. "I was thinking about *her,* that's all."

"Your woman from the ball?" she asked slowly.

"She's driving me crazy," he muttered. "I'm sorry. I didn't mean to bring her up again. I wish I could forget her. But I can't seem to get her off my mind."

"I guess—" C.J. broke off, but started again, with more of an edge this time. "I guess I find it a little hard to believe that you're so enamored of a woman you met only once. I mean, you don't know her name, or anything about her. Why are you so fascinated?"

"I don't know." He wished he had an answer. "It was just so right between us. We talked and we danced and . . . I've never felt that way before."

"You said she was beautiful." C.J.'s voice had become more subdued. "Is that why?"

"Part of it, I suppose."

"Isn't that a pretty shallow attitude, basing all these feelings on what she looked like?" She hugged herself, and her loose blouse drifted off one shoulder, exposing a few inches of pale, creamy skin.

Rowan forced his eyes away. He raked a hand through his hair. "But I really felt something for her," he said hastily. Who was he trying to convince? If he'd felt that way, then why were his eyes pulled back to the curve of Clementine's bare shoulder? Her skin looked as smooth and as soft as the finest porcelain.

"Perfect," he said out loud. "She was just... perfect."

"You and your flyers and your pictures in the paper," C.J. muttered. "You're not going to give up on her, are you?"

He pulled himself together. "No, I'm not," he said grimly. "Once I start something, I don't give up."

He glanced over at C.J., realizing for the first time how she must have been feeling. Here he was, extolling the virtues of another woman while she sat and listened. "I'm sorry," he mumbled. "I don't think we should talk about this anymore."

There was a stubborn cast to C.J.'s chin as she stood up and brushed grass off her jeans. "I don't, either," she said tersely. "In fact, this is the last thing in the world I want to talk about."

"Clementine—" he began, but she cut him off.

"Look," she announced, "I have to get out of here. Karla is headed this way, and I refuse to stick around and deal with her. I guess you'll have to save yourself this time."

And then C.J. took off across the park, leaving him with nothing but a very nice view of her retreating backside. He groaned. The tight white jeans hugged her curvy little bottom like nobody's business, and he felt as if he needed his head examined for not running after her and bringing her back.

But what could he say? He might have been hot for her, but she knew very well he was even hotter for somebody else.

What was happening to him? Was he going crazy? Had this vacation trip to the middle of nowhere so warped him that *everybody* was starting to look good?

It seemed impossible. He'd dated hundreds of beautiful women in his time, and none of them had gotten his blood boiling like this. And now, in Sparks, Wisconsin, where they didn't even have a decent pizza place, he'd run across two of the most tempting females he'd ever seen.

He was losing his mind. That's all there was to it.

"OH, YES, I completely agree," Miss Pru said sagely, as she let them both in the back door to her house. "You must see him again. The poor boy is beside himself with worry, wondering where his dream girl got to. It's only right to alleviate his anxiety."

C.J. glanced over to see if Miss Pru was putting her on, but her sweet little friend seemed completely serious. "It's not because I fell for him or anything," C.J. maintained. "It's not like I'm being drawn back, like I can't stay away. And it's not that I'm jealous of her. A person can't be jealous of herself. So it's nothing like that."

"No, no, of course not."

"It's just that he has to stop making a spectacle of her, well, that is, *me*. He has to stop sending out pictures. Or flyers. It all has to stop."

She shuddered at the very idea of some composite sketch, which would probably make her look like E.T., being scattered all over the state. It was humiliating. And the only way she could think of to head it off was to stage a return visit from Cinderella. Maybe he would discover he wasn't so enamored of her, after all. Or maybe *she* could persuade him to cease and desist.

"He has to stop," she repeated for emphasis.

"Of course he does."

"So you'll help me?"

"Of course I will." Miss Pru beamed at her. "Would you like a day dress or evening wear? And we'd better start heating up the curling tongs, hadn't we?"

"Oh, dear," C.J. said, as she watched Miss Pru positively bounce upstairs to the attic. "I think I've created a monster."

An hour later, she was sure of it. Although her elderly friend maintained this outfit was perfect on her, C.J. felt utterly foolish. It was one thing to go traipsing out in a silly costume under cover of darkness, but in the bright light of a summer afternoon, it was quite another.

She had on a flouncy white dress, with bell-shaped sleeves and a rose at the waist, that Miss Pru recalled had come straight from Paris in 1915. "Only worn once," she explained, "to my older sister Louisa's summer cotillion."

The fine lawn fabric was rather see-through, so they'd found a pretty camisole and petticoat to go underneath it. There was also a big, flat white straw hat with cherries on it, short white gloves, and, of all things, a parasol. With full makeup, and springy curls arranged neatly down her shoulders, she felt like some silent film star, on her way to be tied to the railroad tracks.

Meanwhile, Miss Pru was searching the trunks for the proper white silk stockings and earbobs.

"I can't," C.J. said flatly. After tugging off the hat and the gloves, she began wriggling out of the dress, as well.

"But, my dear, you must!"

"I'm sorry, Miss Pru, but even for Cinderella, this is a bit excessive." She handed over the rejected items. "We don't want to scare the poor man into thinking he's seeing a ghost, or maybe that he fell into some time warp."

"But what will you wear? We agreed there was nothing suitable in your own wardrobe, nothing that would keep you from being recognized."

"I don't know," she said, glancing down at the picture she made standing there in turn-of-the-century underwear. She expected to laugh at herself. Instead she murmured, "You know, this isn't too bad."

She gave herself the once-over in the mirror they'd brought up for the impromptu fashion show. The simple white cotton camisole and calf-length petticoat looked a lot more like modern clothing than anything else she'd tried on, but with enough lace and embroidered touches to have a hint of romance from an earlier age. It would be cool enough to pass muster in the sticky July heat. And yet it was certainly no outfit the regular old C.J. would wear, so it wasn't suspect on that score, either.

"But you can't possibly be seen in your undergarments!" Miss Pru protested.

"It's very cute, don't you think?"

She had a pair of thin sandals at home that she thought would go just fine, and if she put the gloves back on, she could forgo her fake nails, some of which were still scattered on the floorboards of her truck.

"Let him think I have warts or something," she muttered.

"Warts?" Miss Pru echoed, horrified. "Whatever do you mean?"

"Nothing, sweetheart. Don't worry about it." She spun one more time to be sure she liked it. "I think we've got it."

C.J. brushed the ringlets out of her hair, leaving it full, but not too curly, hitching the sides back with some ivory combs Miss Pru provided. "Oh!" she said suddenly. "My eyes! Miss Pru, what am I going to do about my eyes? Even if I wear the contacts, he'll recognize me. But I can't wear a mask this time! What will I do?"

"How about the hat?" her friend suggested, holding it and its bobbing cherries up for inspection.

"No, that won't do. I always wear hats. Not like that, but still... He knows what I look like under a hat."

"Yes, I suppose you're right." Miss Pru fussed and poked through a tray in one of the trunks, finally holding up a lorgnette, a pair of old-fashioned, bejeweled spectacles with a long handle. "Perhaps something like this?"

"No," C.J. said slowly. "Not quite."

But the idea was right. Glasses. As in sunglasses. Karla had been wearing a pair of red sunglasses. Why not Cinderella?

"I have a pair of big, dark sunglasses I got once when I went to Mexico. They'll be perfect. So all I have to do is go home to get the right shoes and my glasses, and then I'm off." After quickly donning her tennis shoes, she stopped and kissed Miss Pru on the cheek, then dashed to the attic stairs. But on the top step, she hesitated. "He'd better still be there."

"Oh, he will. I'm sure of it." Miss Pru's smile was very encouraging. "He won't leave before the fireworks."

"More fireworks?" she asked, remembering what had happened the last time.

"Of course! It is Independence Day, after all. What would it be without fireworks?"

"I wouldn't worry about it, Miss Pru." One way or another, C.J. felt very sure there were going to be fireworks.

"You'd better give me a full report, young lady," Miss Pru called after her. "Are you sure you shouldn't take a wrap?"

But Cinderella was off to the remnants of the Fourth of July picnic, and she had no time to worry about jackets.

"OH, THERE YOU ARE, Rowan!" Karla Farley squealed, clamping a big red picture hat firmly to her head as she raced toward him. Teetering on platform sandals, she called out, "I've been looking for you all day!"

He was aware of that. And he'd been doing his best to avoid her without turning it into a slapstick routine. He'd thought he was a goner the last time, after C.J. had left him alone under the oak tree. But then at the last minute, Darla had caught up to Karla, squawking something about who had first dibs on *him* for the picnic. He shuddered just thinking about it, but at least their subsequent squabble had given him just enough time to sneak around behind a bush and out of their range.

He supposed eluding Karla forever was too much to hope for. Standing at the back of the pavilion, near the jugs of lemonade, he was afraid she'd finally caught up with him. He backed up as far as he could go, but then he hit the wall of the pavilion.

"Trapped," he said under his breath.

"Don't try to sweet-talk me, you naughty boy!"

He gave her a baffled stare. What in the hell was she talking about? God forbid he should try to sweet-talk her!

"I saw you with that horrible C. J. Bede," she cooed, in a sort of silly singsong voice, as she clutched at him with a fistful of scarlet fingernails. "I thought you were so antsy to find that silly woman in the paper, and that was bad enough, but now you've gone from bad to worse. *Now* you're letting yourself be seen with that horrible Bede girl. Rowan, what will people think?"

"Why should people think anything?" he asked, ducking out from under her hands and putting a picnic table in between them. He didn't really care what she said—or who thought what, for that matter—but he figured there was a chance a little loose gossip would clue him in on C.J. and her mysterious relationship to the rest of the town.

"Because... Well, because those Bedes are a no-good family and always have been, and she's just the latest spawn in their trashy parade."

Her words were so hurtful, and so casually uttered, that he found himself wanting to slap her. Since when had he turned into an avenger of maligned young ladies? He stuck his neck out for nobody. C.J.'s reputation was nothing to him.

Nonetheless, he had to bite down to keep from lashing out at Karla. "I find it very difficult to believe that C.J. ever did anything that she wasn't provoked to do," he said roughly.

"Huh! And I suppose she didn't throw up at my Sweet Sixteen party and ruin everything?"

He stared at her in disbelief. "This town treats her and her mother like pariahs because Clementine threw up at your Sweet Sixteen party? You've got to be kidding."

"Well, there's more," Karla blustered. "Plenty more. It's just that I'm too much of a lady to speak of it."

Uh-huh. And he was Mickey Mouse. He turned to go, not even bothering with an exit line.

"So why do you care, anyway?" Karla demanded. "I thought you were so all-fired hot to find that Cinderella girl. But now you seem fascinated with Clemmy Bede, of all people. Why, it's positively disgusting! Which one do you want, anyway?"

He'd been wondering the same thing. He just didn't want to deal with it.

Rowan had felt certain that C.J. was a curiosity, nothing more. He'd told himself that he simply found her and her insolent attitude unusual. Most people bent over backward to be nice to someone who had as many bucks in the bank as he did. But she didn't. And he'd wanted to know why.

So he'd figured he would ask a few questions, solve the puzzle that was Clementine and that would be that.

But it had turned into more. When she shot insults at him, accused him of being a pirate, told him he was shallow, it made him want to behave better to earn her respect.

"That's crazy," he whispered. What did he care what she thought?

But he did care. And when her blouse slipped off her shoulder, when her eyes lit up with pleasure, when her jeans hugged her bottom, he found he wanted more than just her respect.

He wanted her body, he wanted her mind, he wanted her soul.

"Oh no," he groaned. Once he admitted that, what did it say for his wonderful woman in white?

Moodily he realized he didn't know. That night at the ball, his mystery woman had touched something deep inside him, some crazy romantic streak he didn't realize he had. He'd felt out of control, over his head, afraid to touch her, afraid not to. In his imagination, she was excruciatingly real, and at the same time, as hazy and ephemeral as a midnight dream.

It was as if she represented something he'd never had, something he'd never been aware he was missing. Once he'd met her, danced with her, held her in his arms, he'd felt so sure he could never live without it—without her—again.

C.J. was common sense, laughter, someone he could talk to, someone who demanded the best of him.

Cinderella was drama, excitement, a crazy dream of music and romance.

C.J. was a woman.

Cinderella was an angel.

Which one did he choose? Did he even have the opportunity to choose?

Rowan's hand curled into a fist around that half a bottle rocket he still kept in his pocket. What in the hell was he going to do?

He was half in love with two women, or maybe all in love with half of each of them. Like the little firecracker party favor that had fitted so neatly, one of these women was the other half of him. But he had no idea which one.

"Rowan!" Karla said loudly, tapping him on the shoulder. "Hellooo? Earth to Rowan!"

He couldn't keep the annoyance from his voice. When he was thinking about his dream woman, he didn't need Karla barking at him and wrecking the fantasy. "What?" he demanded.

"Well, you don't need to get so snappy about it. It's common courtesy to listen when a person is talking to you, y' know."

Before Rowan had a chance to reply, he was clapped on the back, and then collared like a steer in a roping contest. Buzz Farley had sneaked up on him, yoking him and Karla together in a hearty hug. Karla's hat fell off to one side, and she started to giggle, while Buzz chuckled and announced, "Are you two kids havin' fun?" as he bounced them together.

Rowan felt his temper begin to rise. He didn't like being breathed on, leaned over, squeezed, grabbed or patted. He hated having his cheeks pinched, his hair tousled and his back slapped. But he especially despised this sort of jolly, overwhelming bear hug when it was coming from someone he barely knew.

It took every ounce of strength he had not to knock Buzz's block off. After prying Buzz's meaty fist off his shoulder, Rowan wrenched himself loose, grabbing Buzz by the collar and lifting him slightly, threateningly. "Keep your hands to yourself." And then he dropped the old buffoon back on his heels.

Karla's mouth fell open. "But, Rowan, you don't want to be mean to my daddy. Everybody knows it's important to stay on my daddy's good side. Why, he's the biggest man in this town!"

Rowan smiled thinly. "Not since I got here."

With visions of losing his factory clearly dancing in his simple mind, Buzz went white. "Karla, go tell the boy what's what. Don't want him going off mad," he said hastily, pushing his daughter, almost toppling her completely on her wobbly shoes.

Rowan shook his head with disgust. Forget subtlety or good manners. He'd had enough of the Farleys to last him a lifetime, and he didn't care who knew it.

"Buzz," he icily, "I have no intention of going anywhere near your daughters *or* your factory. Call off the dogs."

"What's that supposed to mean?" Karla shouted. "Daddy, I think he insulted me."

"Good guess," Rowan muttered, jamming his hands in his pockets. He turned and stalked away from the pavilion, needing a little distance in between him and the Farleys.

Behind him, Karla shouted, "Nobody in this town is gonna give you the time of day after I tell them you're mixed up with that bastard Clemmy Bede!"

"Shut up, Karla," her father commanded, but Rowan spun on his heels.

"What did you call her?"

"A bastard," she said smugly. "As in out-of-wedlock, illegitimate bastard. Because that's what she is."

And suddenly it all made sense. It was the oldest story in the world, and the kind of thing snobs like the Farleys loved to get their teeth into. Rowan shook his head. No wonder C.J. was protective of her mother. No wonder she didn't want him to know.

To Karla, he said quietly, "I happen to respect Clementine a great deal. From everything I've seen, you're not fit to shine her shoes."

And then he started walking, away from them and the rest of the town, until he got to the small lake that formed the centerpiece of the town park. Rowan stood there, hands in his pockets, looking out over the calm, dark water.

He stared out into the deep, indigo water, wondering how in hell he'd come to this. His temper was short, and his mood was worse. He'd baited and bedeviled a woman he'd ended up liking very much, finally stumbling across her secret when it was none of his business. And then he'd verbally abused the town's biggest businessman just for sport, coming within a hairbreadth of punching him *and* his daughter.

The chilly, unflappable Prince of Takeovers, the one who never got mad, only got even, the one who didn't turn a hair when millions were on the line, was just about to blow sky high. Here he was, seething and fuming, restless and tense.

And he knew why.

Even before he turned, he knew she would be there. And she was.

His Cinderella had returned. And he was more confused than ever.

Chapter Eight

It was as if there was something in the air, some hint of perfume on the sultry breeze.

"Is it really you?" he whispered, as his heart hammered against his ribs. A fierce sense of joy flooded through him. He wasn't crazy. She did exist. "Thank God."

She was as graceful, as lovely, as he remembered, slowly making her way down the path to where he stood at the edge of the lake. Her long blond hair was swept back on the sides, away from her face, although oversize dark glasses still kept her eyes and much of her expression hidden. His mystery woman was still being mysterious.

But he didn't care. She was back, and that was good enough for now.

Except for the glasses, she was wearing white. Of course she was. White was her color. In the blazing afternoon sun, she seemed to glow with it.

Her arms were bare, but her dress was delicate and old-fashioned looking, with a simple, pretty top, and a full, lace-edged skirt that billowed around her legs in the soft wind. She wore short white gloves, like a

Southern belle at Sunday school. Once again, he had the sensation that she was too fragile and too romantic to come from his own high-speed, high-tech era.

She was also slimmer and less curvy than he'd thought, but now he remembered better. Of course. How could he have forgotten? She was small.

He remembered now how tiny her waist had felt between his hands when they danced, and how slender her shoulders had looked in the daring strapless dress. To see her again, to refresh his recollection, was like a drink of cool water on this hot, murky day. An unexpected gift.

Watching him from behind dark glasses, she hesitated a few feet away. A part of him—the darkest, angriest part—wanted to shake her, to demand why she'd run away, where she'd been and why she hadn't come back to him before this. But he didn't do any of those things.

Instead he let his better instincts rule. Without thinking, he bridged the short distance between them and hauled her into his arms.

"I can't believe it," he murmured, pulling her closer still, wrapping himself around her as he lifted her into the air. "You're really here."

Setting her down, he ran his hands over the thin cotton of her dress. Even through the cool fabric, she felt warm and alive...and real. Astonishingly real. He'd almost convinced himself she was only a fantasy.

"I need to—" she began, in that hot, husky little voice that unwound whatever good intentions he had left.

"I don't care what you need," he said roughly. At the moment, what *he* needed would have to do for both of them.

Before she had a chance to say another word, he framed her face in his hands and fastened his mouth over hers. He was so hungry to taste her, to fill his emptiness with as much of her as he could get. He heard the greedy little noise she made at the same time her arms wound around his neck, and he knew she was as eager as he was.

Harder he pressed, and deeper he delved, losing his bruised ego and his anger, finding only their combined passion, their combined heat. Her mouth was wet and welcoming under his, and her little white gloves felt positively sinful rubbing against his neck, ruffling the edges of his hair. He'd never kissed anyone like this, like this mingling of minds and bodies and souls, and he wasn't sure he could handle ever doing it again.

Taking a breath, he found himself smiling like a crazy man, or maybe just a drunken one. "I don't where you've been, but I'm definitely not letting you go this time."

And then he found her mouth again, selfishly, as if marking his territory.

"Wait, wait," she cried, but he kissed the corners of her lips and the fine line of her chin, nuzzling her neck as she went limp in his arms. "Please," she whispered, "I didn't come here for this."

"I don't care why you came." He felt reckless, giddy. He'd found her! More precisely, she'd found him, but he wasn't about to quibble. "You're here now, and that's all that matters."

"No, it's not." He could tell she was reluctant. She pushed back, away from his embrace, and then made a point of fussing with her sunglasses, as if making sure they hadn't fallen out of place. "I—I have to talk to you…"

He slipped a hand to her waist, trying to persuade her to come back a little closer. "We're talking, aren't we?"

"No," she said plainly. She held him at arms' length. "You're kissing me, and I'm forgetting all my good intentions."

But she smiled as she said it. Had he ever seen her smile? It was breathtaking, offering that peculiar mix of innocent and siren that drove him wild. Her smile, her words, her intonation, reminded him of someone. Someone he knew…

No. This was impossible. She was starting to remind him of C.J.!

Quickly he forced the thought out of his mind. With his dream woman in his arms, he was sure which one he loved. This one.

"I was beginning to doubt my sanity," he admitted. "But then I saw the picture from the ball, and I knew you were real. God, if you only knew what you've put me through."

"That's what I want to talk to you about," she said quickly. "Those pictures. In the paper, I mean. You have to stop putting my picture in the paper."

"So you saw it?"

"Of course. How could I miss? Everyone saw it. Those pictures were everywhere!"

"But why didn't anyone tell me who you were when they saw your picture?" Rowan demanded, remembering how frustrated and upset he'd been ever since she'd disappeared so ignominiously. "How could everyone in the world leave me hanging?"

"I'm so sorry." Her gloved hand brushed his cheek, and he caught it and held it there. "I never intended to... I mean, I just wanted to..."

At her obvious distress, he relented. He pressed a small kiss into the bare skin near her wrist. "It doesn't matter."

"Yes, it does." Breaking the connection between them, she edged away, gazing off into the lake. Even with the dark sunglasses, he knew her expression was miserable. "It's just that...well, they knew, but I'm not sure they knew they knew, if you know what I mean." She broke off. "It's complicated."

"I don't understand."

Her low, sultry voice took on a new note of urgency. "I'm begging you to stop this hunt of yours. With the pictures and the questions...you have to stop."

"But I won't need to go on now," he assured her.

"Then you'll promise me that there will be no more pictures, no more investigations?"

With her here, he would've promised anything. "Of course."

"Say the words."

"I promise." He smiled, trying to lighten the mood. "Why would I need to go on looking? I've found you."

There was a long pause. "But I can't stay," she said awkwardly. "I thought you realized."

When he started to speak, to protest, she went on in a rush. "I only came to tell you that you can't go on with this search of yours, that you're making things impossible for me. I was hoping you'd understand.''

"But I don't understand. We belong together. Surely you know that now."

And then she started to laugh. He couldn't believe it. Rowan McKenna, the Wall Street Wunderkind, was pouring out his heart to a woman for the first time in his life, practically begging her not to leave him, and she had the unmitigated gall to laugh at him.

"What's so damn funny?" he growled.

She held her gloved hand over her mouth, as if holding back her laughter. "You. You're out of your mind."

"I already knew that. I'd have to be to mess around with you."

"You don't even know me," she told him in a mocking tone. "'We belong together,' you say. And yet you don't know my name, or where I live, or the slightest thing about me. So how can you stand there, with those beautiful blue eyes of yours shining with sincerity, and tell me we belong together?"

"At least you know what color they are."

"Which is more than I can say for you."

Her tone—her whole voice—had changed. She sounded aggravated and annoyed, as if the idea that he didn't know her eye color was a major problem. "But I do," he assured her. He found a lazy, crooked smile just for her. "How could I forget your eyes? They're violet. And they're stunning."

"That's ex ..." she began, but she caught herself, and when she spoke again, the deeper, huskier, slower voice was back in place. "Eye color is the least of it,

Mr. McKenna. We both know I'm right. You don't know me at all."

He was beginning to think she *was* right. How and why had her voice altered like that? He narrowed his gaze, even as he told himself that he knew all he needed to.

Hands in his pockets, he fingered his half of that damn bottle rocket, the thing that had convinced him in the first place just how right, how fated it was for them to be together.

"It has to be," he said out loud. He took her hand and raised it once more to his lips, lingering there, peeling back her glove far enough to drop a soft kiss across the back of her hand. Somehow it was more erotic than it would've been if her hand were bare to begin with. "From the first moment I saw you, I knew you belonged with me. That hasn't changed."

"No?" She turned away again, into the sun, so that sunshine splashed the top of her golden head and lit up her profile. "I thought maybe you would've changed your mind."

He felt sure, all of a sudden, that she knew he had been dallying with C.J. in her absence. "Nothing can change my mind," he said quickly.

Slowly she asked, "And what if I have seven kids stashed in a shoe somewhere? Does that change anything?"

"Do you?"

She hesitated. "No, no. I don't. But still—"

He smiled. "I didn't think so."

"Well, then, what about a husband?" she demanded. She fiddled with the edge of her glove, where he could see that his mouth had left the heavy cotton slightly damp. "Did it occur to you that I might already be taken?"

"Oh, yes, it occurred to me."

"And?"

"You weren't wearing a wedding ring at the ball. You're not wearing one now."

"But the gloves..."

"I would've felt it through the glove."

But she shook her head. "Not everyone wears a wedding ring. Especially if I were going out to cheat on my husband, I'd take it off."

"I suppose you would." He watched her, waiting for her reaction. "But it doesn't matter, one way or the other. Husbands are easily disposed of."

That took her aback. Even through the dark glasses, he knew she was staring. "Disposed of?"

"Gotten rid of. Taken care of." He shrugged. "Whatever."

"Are you talking about cement overshoes and a trip to the bottom of Lake Michigan?" she asked in a strangulated voice.

He tried to act serious, but he suspected there was a twinkle in his eye. "Not unless it's absolutely necessary."

His mysterious woman in white shook her head, letting the long waves of her hair spill down over her shoulders. "You're very cold, you know that? Joking about murdering some imaginary husband, like it was nothing."

"Imaginary?"

There was a pause. "That's right. Imaginary. I'm not married."

He felt relief swamp him, but he held on, unwilling to let her see how much the information meant to him. "I'm glad to hear that," he said carefully.

"I wouldn't have come to the ball, and I wouldn't have kissed you. If I were married or engaged . . . or anything."

Intuitively he'd known that about her, even if he'd doubted his faith on occasion. "I know."

"Good." She hazarded a glance his way. "You wouldn't really have gotten rid of anyone, would you? If there had been someone, I mean."

"If they stood in my way, yes, I would," he said quietly. "I was talking about getting you a divorce or a separation, or whatever suited you best. But I would have no compunction about excising another man from your life. None."

"You're crazy," she whispered. "Absolutely stark raving mad."

"I know what I want and I go after it."

"But you're talking divorces and separations, for a woman whose name you don't even know!"

"That's easily remedied. Tell me."

But she shook her head. "I can't."

Rowan caught her hand, drawing her closer. "I let you disappear from the ball, and I let you show up here, no questions asked. Didn't I?"

Slowly she nodded.

"But now you have to tell me your name." Her lips parted; he could tell she was trying to put together an argument. But he put a finger across her lips, impeding her words, and at the same time he angled closer. Much closer. Seductively, persuasively, he urged, "Just your name. Nothing else. That's all I want."

A ghost of a smile played across her lips. "That's not all you want."

"No, it isn't. But it's a start."

"I can't," she said again, softer but more sure.

"Yes, you can." He dipped his mouth to the slope of her neck, nibbling gently, and she trembled in response. She was warming up nicely, leaning into his caress, feeling very pliant and very agreeable. He was going to win. He knew it. "Tell me."

Her voice was barely a whisper. "No."

"Yes."

She shook her head slightly, but it only lifted her ear closer to his mouth, and her delectable body more firmly into his embrace.

He was heating up himself, and he had to slow down or risk losing control completely. But she was so tempting, so willing. And for this one moment in time, she was all his. He'd been trying to tantalize her into giving him the information he wanted, but he seriously wondered who was seducing whom here.

"Your name," he coaxed, easing her up against him.

She gave no answer.

"Your name," he repeated, sliding one hand up, ever so gently, to graze the cool fabric of her dress where it swelled over her breast, and the other down, ever so slightly, rounding the curve of her beautiful little bottom.

"Your name," he whispered, brushing his thumb over the nipple he could feel rising to greet him through the pristine cotton.

But she didn't answer. All she did was make an incoherent little moan that sent new flames of desire licking over his body. He was already rock hard, and he'd barely touched her.

"Tell me your name," he said fiercely, trying to rein himself in. But her breast was warm and perfect under his hand, and he couldn't resist teasing that impudent little nipple. Again, it felt more erotic to play the game his way, to take his time, to touch her and taunt her through the fabric.

Although he couldn't quite resist the mental image of ripping away the buttons down the front of her pretty little blouse, tearing away the cloth and baring her soft flesh to his hungry gaze.

He knew, from somewhere deep within, what her skin would feel like under his fingers, and what she would taste like when he lowered his head and flicked his tongue...

He groaned. "Please tell me. Please. I have to know."

"No, Rowan." This time, there was real fear in her voice, and she stiffened in his arms. "Don't ask me again, or I will leave you here again, all by yourself."

"But why?"

"I can't tell you," she said again. "I promise you, that if I could, if I did, it would ruin everything. You wouldn't want me anymore."

He didn't understand. What she said made no sense to him, as if she were speaking in riddles. And he felt his temper begin to flare. "This is nonsense," he told her harshly. "If there's someone hurting you, or holding you back, I told you—they will no longer exist. Whatever the problem is, I can fix it."

But she was as stubborn as he. "The problem is me. You can't fix that. Not even you."

"Let me try."

But she shook her head. "If you push me, I will have to leave, do you understand? I won't have a choice."

"I don't want you to go."

"I don't want to go, either. Not yet. Not when things are like this between us."

"I won't let you."

She said softly, "You can't stop me."

And he knew it was true. If she really wanted to run away, just as she had before, there was no way in the world for him to stop her.

Except one. He smiled with the arrogance of a man who knows when a woman is completely his.

"No way?"

And he kissed her, full and deep, branding her with all the frustration and the rage he still felt over the abrupt end to their first encounter, with all his new irritation from her continued woman-of-mystery routine. It was hard and hot this time, no meeting of minds, just a clash of wills and a violent storm of passion, until finally they had to break away to take in some air.

Breathing raggedly, he clasped her shoulders hard, holding her away. He said savagely, "I still want you, whatever your name is. But I will find out what this game is all about. You know I will."

"This is no game," she returned. And then she kissed him back.

She was as brutal and as single-minded as he had been, wrapping her arms around his neck to drag him down to her. As she hit him with everything she had,

opening her mouth to him, urging him inside, she also
held him so close, fitting her body to his.

He buried his hands in her hair, and he lost himself
in that endless, terrible kiss. As ferocious as it was, it
felt better than anything he could possibly have imagined. Her softness imprinted itself on his harder
frame, and he knew he would never forget the feel of
her as long as he lived.

If this was a challenge, he was more than up to it.
He picked her up, completely off the ground, guiding
them both to a grassy bank where they could pursue
this fiery duel in more comfort.

But when he set her down on the grass, intending to
follow, something changed. He saw her tousled hair,
with one comb completely missing, and the other
hanging loose; her love-swollen lips; and the ripped
lace at the neckline of her top. Her skirt was all askew,
revealing long, bare legs that his fingers ached to ex-
plore. But he knew better.

Dammit. He *was* better than this, than some quick,
angry tumble on the grass. He might be mad, and she
might be the most infuriating woman he'd ever met,
but he wasn't going to make love with her like this.

"What's wrong?" she asked suddenly.

But he just stood there. Finally he said softly, "Are
you my dream woman? Or my worst nightmare?"

"I don't know."

"I don't know, either, but I do know this is not the
way it should be between you and me." He reached
into his pocket, pulling out and holding up the little
bottle rocket that had started it all. "We're supposed
to be about dreams, about two people who fit to-

gether so well they're like the two halves of this damn puzzle. The way it was that night . . ."

"I know," she whispered. "I know. But that was make-believe. We're real people, not characters in a fairy tale."

"You've made that abundantly clear," he said, with a sarcastic edge that made her wince.

"So what do you want from me?"

"I want *you,*" he said simply. "The real you. Take off the damn glasses, and tell me now who you are and what this is all about. We can still make it work."

She moistened her lips with her tongue, hesitating, obviously deciding. But then she said, "No, I can't. I have to finish something. It's taken me too long to get this far, and it's just too important. I can't ruin everything now."

"I don't know what you're talking about."

She lifted her chin. "That's the way it has to be." Brushing off her skirt, she rose and started to go.

"Wait." His voice was the only thing holding her, but miraculously, she stayed. "You made me promise not to look for you anymore."

"Yes."

"I'll keep that promise." He saw her evident relief. "But I'll need one from you in return."

Once again, she paused. "What is it?"

He knew he was behaving like a lunatic. She was nothing but trouble, and he should make her promise to stay far, far away.

But he needed to see her again. He had to.

If he had one more chance, maybe he could persuade her to open up to him, to let him in on whatever her huge, horrible secret was. He couldn't let this end without one more encounter, however brief, however unsatisfying. Hell, it couldn't be worse than this one.

His words were slow and measured. "I want you to promise to come back to me one more time. If you'll promise, I'll take your picture out of the paper."

"And the sketch artist? And the flyers?"

He went very still. "How do you know about that?"

Silence separated them.

"Forget it." He dismissed it with an impatient wave of his hand. "You've made it clear you're not going to tell me anything that might be useful." He could sort out who he'd told and who he hadn't on his own, and try to see if that helped him identify her. He doubted it. "What about the promise?" he prompted.

She bent over, kicking her toe into the grass, and her flowing hair obscured her face even more. "I would come to you, somewhere here in town, whenever I choose. One visit. Is that all there is to it?"

"No."

A short laugh escaped her. "Somehow I didn't think so." She sighed. "So what's the catch?"

"No glasses, no mask. Just you. Come to my house, the place I'm renting outside of town. You can come whenever you want to, but you'll stay as long as *I* want you to."

"And if I say yes, you'll stop all of it—the photos and the questions—everything?"

"Yes."

She thought for a moment, but he knew the final decision was made on the spur of the moment, against her better judgment. "Okay," she said quickly. "At your house. You can expect me."

And then she turned and fled quickly up the path and into the cover of tall pines and birches. Her dress was a flash of white for a few moments before she disappeared completely.

"Well, McKenna," he said out loud. "You are a damn fool. That woman is as crazy as a loon. And if she's not, you are." He smiled, searching for a stick or a rock to throw into the lake. "Damned if we're not a perfect match."

Chapter Nine

C.J. was as nervous as a cat. Since her own cat, Samantha, was currently snoozing peacefully, looking like a a boneless puddle of fur, C.J. figured she was a lot more nervous than at least one cat in the world.

She shoved her drawer shut, putting her half of that silly bottle rocket safely out of view, and then she got out from behind her desk, determined to do some work and behave more constructively. But what she ended up doing was pacing back and forth in front of her desk, trying to figure out what she was going to do about the mess she'd gotten herself into. For a very sensible woman, she was in a very deep, dark hole.

With a muttered oath, she pulled off her trusty baseball cap—this one advertised the Chicago Bulls—and slapped it down on her desk so hard that it bounced over and underneath the desk, into oblivion. Swell.

Verbally berating herself, she ran her fingers through her hair and rubbed her temples. Suddenly neither her beloved barns nor her long-sought revenge seemed important in the least. With every beat of her heart, thoughts of one thing and one thing only pounded through her brain. Him.

When would she see him again? What would he do or say this time? How could she possibly continue to hold her own?

She'd promised a return appearance, but how could she risk another visit? On the other hand, how could she stay away?

C.J. was more confused and upset than she'd ever been before, more even than the fateful day she'd found out Buzz was her real father. Then she'd been disgusted and violently angry, but she'd known immediately what she would do. She would make him pay.

This time, there was no easy or obvious course of action. She was miserable, and it was her own fault. Of course, it was Rowan McKenna's fault, too, for coming to her town in the first place and throwing a major wrench in the works, but after that, the blame rested squarely on C.J.'s shoulders.

She was the one with the brilliant idea to play masquerade, and the even more ridiculous notion to go for a second round. "What was I thinking?" she asked out loud, almost stepping on the cat.

Samantha shot to her feet, gave C.J. a baleful stare, and then huffily retreated to a safer spot under a chair near the window. As the cat circled around, staking out her place, C.J. stewed.

No matter what she started out doing, she ended up staring into space and wondering about *him*. What was he doing? Was he thinking about her? Was he keeping his promise, or was he still looking for her, still hatching schemes to uncover her identity and ruin her life?

"Damn that man!" she swore loudly. "Why did he have to come here? Of all the gin joints in all the towns in all the world, and he walks into mine."

She was paraphrasing a line from the movie *Casablanca*, but it seemed to relate perfectly to her current hopeless situation.

"Who are you talking to?" someone asked from the direction of her front door, and C.J. whirled.

It was only Rainy Day Delmar, the teen queen who worked at Petticoat Junction in town, but C.J.'s pulse was racing. What had she been muttering about? Had she given anything away? Suddenly she longed for the days when she could speak her mind without worrying that someone else might overhear a minor comment and shout, "Aha! You are unmasked!"

"You scared me," she said finally, twisting her hair back into a ponytail and searching on her desk for a rubber band. "I didn't hear the door open. What can I do for you, Rainy Day?"

The girl sidled herself and her skin-tight jeans skirt farther into the office, pulling a huge tapestried purse in behind her. "I, um, kind of need a favor. I was hoping you'd help me."

"Me? What can I help you with?"

"The pageant," Rainy Day said hopefully. "I need a little help with the talent part. See, I'm doing this drama thing."

"A drama thing?"

"Uh-huh. A dramatic reading. From *Charlotte's Web*. You know, with the spider and the pig."

"I vaguely remember it," C.J. said weakly. It sounded positively awful. Of course, the competition would no doubt be playing "Stairway to Heaven" on the xylophone, or tap-dancing on stilts, so Rainy Day would fit right in.

"I need a backdrop," the would-be beauty queen explained. "I'm supposed to look like I'm in Charlotte's barn. Well, I guess it's Wilbur's barn, isn't it? But, anyway, I thought maybe you could make me some kind of little barn thing to go behind me when I do it."

"I see. It involves a barn, so you thought of me." C.J. smiled in spite of herself. "Lucky me."

"It would be so cool," Rainy Day assured her. "And I know it wouldn't be hard at all. Just the front of a barn, to come down behind me when I come out, like, boom! There it is."

"Did you think of asking someone at the high school? Someone in the drama department, maybe?"

"Oh, I can't!" she returned, with enough melodrama to make C.J. think maybe she did have possibilities as an actress. "Cherise Dunlap is also in the contest, and she's like Miss Number-One Big Actress at school. The drama teacher is helping her rig up some totally cool thing. So I need something even cooler if I'm going to beat her."

She could feel herself weakening. She always had had a soft spot for underdogs. Besides, Rainy Day was the one who'd complimented her figure and told her she could wipe up the competition in an evening gown. C.J. smiled. Nobody else had ever told her that.

"Your barns are so totally cool, and I know you're really smart," Rainy Day said, her wide blue eyes shining with sincerity. "I know you could help me win, C.J."

"Well, maybe..." she mused. "When is this thing?"

"Friday night."

"Friday? But that's only three days."

"I know. And I also need a big spiderweb, with a spider on it. And a pig."

God help her, she was actually considering it. Certainly her artistic and construction talents were up to the task. In fact, it would be a piece of cake, even if there were only three days.

And then there was the fact that it involved the Miss Firecracker pageant. She'd never seen it up close, never even been to one, and she'd always had a secret hankering to.

Although she'd never told anyone, she knew that way back when, her very own mother had won the Miss Firecracker title. It was hard to imagine now, but C.J. had seen the pictures and the crown tucked away in a box under the bed, so she knew it was true. *Ivy Bede, Miss Firecracker 1959.* She wondered what her mother's talent had been. How funny that she'd never thought to ask.

It would also give her something to think about that did not include Rowan McKenna.

"Okay," C.J. said quickly. "Let's go for it. Can you get me into the theater tonight, so I can see the space?"

"We have a rehearsal tonight..." Rainy Day rummaged around in her cavernous purse for something with the time on it, but she was so excited that she was almost jumping up and down. "This is going to be so great!" she kept saying. And then, in a burst of spontaneity, she reached over and hugged C.J. "You're going to be so good at this," she bubbled. "I just know we're going to win!"

C.J. didn't quite know how to handle this. It seemed she'd made a friend of a teenage girl, and that was a new phenomenon. Except for Miss Pru, C.J. had always had male friends. The girls in high school and the women in college had always been so wrapped up in makeup and men that she'd felt inadequate by comparison. So what was she going to do with Rainy Day Delmar and her effusive new friendship?

"What's going on? I could hear giggling all the way outside."

There he was. He'd wedged his big, beautiful body back inside her office and her life when she wasn't looking, and she felt as if she'd been hit over the head with a brick. C.J. rushed to get out from under her new pal's hug. As soon as she disengaged herself from Rainy Day, she retreated to the safety of her antique dentist's chair and then stuck her head down under her desk. She knew her missing baseball cap had to be down there somewhere, and she wasn't coming out until she was properly dressed as herself again.

"Oh, wow!"

From the tone of Rainy Day's voice, C.J. could tell the kid was very impressed with the charming Prince of Takeovers. As C.J. came out from under the desk, hat firmly in place down over her eyes, Rainy Day backed toward the door, hauling her purse with her. He was in the doorway, and that's where the bouncy teenager also wanted to go, so she tried to squeeze around him, but ended up sideswiping him with the big tapestry bag. And then, as he attempted to get out of her way, she accidentally bashed him again. Poor Rowan let out a yelp of pain.

"Oh, I'm so sorry! Really!" the girl lamented. "And you're a judge! I haven't even done my prepageant interview yet, and I've already wounded one of the judges!"

"You're a judge?" C.J. asked faintly.

She could only hope that judges and set-builders would not occupy the same space at any point. Even with the protective buffer of Rainy Day, C.J. felt her whole body jump into alert the minute he came into the room. Her toes started to tingle and her hands started to perspire, and she couldn't think of anything to do with either of them.

It had only been yesterday when Rowan had stripped back her glove and pressed his lips to the back of that very same hand. Shaking it as if it were on fire, C.J. glanced down, jumped and stuck her shaking hand into her jeans pocket.

"Is there something wrong with your hand?"

"No, of course not."

There was a long pause as he waited for her to elaborate. But she felt the best action at this point might be no action, so she clamped her mouth shut and sat down abruptly in her dentist's chair.

"Bye!" Rainy Day called out as she finally cleared the door. "I'll see you tonight, C.J."

"I gather that that young lady is a contestant in the beauty pageant I so rashly agreed to judge," he said dryly.

"Yes."

"And she's a friend of yours?"

Well, she was now. "Yes."

"Are you somehow involved with the pageant?"

"What is this?" she demanded, forgetting she wasn't supposed to talk. "Twenty Questions?"

Rowan smiled, that insufferably arrogant smile he did so well. "Just making conversation."

"You drove all the way out here just to make conversation?"

"Well, no." He shrugged, folding himself into a chair near where Samantha was sleeping. As he bent down to pet the cat, C.J. fully expected hissing and spitting and maybe a good scratch or two. But the cat just yawned and flipped over, letting him rub her tummy. C.J. was stunned. Samantha didn't like anyone.

"I actually came by to apologize," he said, pausing in midrub, eliciting a plaintive meow that sounded like a demand for more. When he didn't oblige, Samantha hopped up in his lap and curled into a contented little ball, further astonishing her mistress. "I didn't like the way our last conversation turned out, and I wanted to make things right if I could."

C.J. tried to remember which last conversation that would be. The one under the oak tree, when she was herself? Or the other one down by the lake, when she was Cinderella?

Her double life was making her head spin.

"Good Lord," she muttered under her breath. "This is getting ridiculous."

Of course it was the one under the oak tree. But what had they said? And what was he apologizing for? Starting rumors that made the stock rise? Dancing under the stars until he mesmerized her? Not recognizing her when she was right in front of him?

That was a big one, but he didn't know he'd done it. Did he? She sat up very straight. Surely if he knew what was what, he wouldn't be making small talk or apologies. He'd be strangling her with his bare hands.

Hopelessly confused, she asked, "What do you have to be sorry for?"

"Your mother."

She blinked twice. "My mother?"

"Karla told me about..." He paused. "About you."

"Karla Farley should just keep her damn mouth shut," she shot back. "That little witch has no right to..." She swallowed. Once again, her mind was racing. How bad was this going to be? What did he know and how long had he known it? "And what did Karla tell you?"

"That you threw up at her Sweet Sixteen party," he said, with a definite spark of mischief.

She hardly thought that was the extent of it. But if he was pussyfooting around, she could figure out why. "And she also told you that I'm illegitimate, didn't she?" She raised her chin, ready to tough it out. "I'm not afraid to say it."

Rowan smiled. If he'd shown the slightest hint of sympathy or pity, she would've cheerfully socked him. But he didn't. Instead his grin was full of a kind of pride and respect that warmed her down to her toes. "Clementine, you are the most legitimate woman I've ever met."

After a moment, she said, "I know."

His smile widened. "I did want to apologize, though." He shrugged, and she got the idea he wasn't used to feeling sheepish. "I kind of plowed ahead into what was none of my business. You told me to stay out, and I didn't listen, and I'm sorry.''

"It's okay," she said sweetly, smiling back at him. "I forgive you."

She hadn't meant to make the words soft and low, like her Cinderella voice, but they came out that way, anyway, and he looked up suddenly, with a slight narrowing of his clear blue eyes.

It was getting impossible to separate her two identities, impossible to remember what distinctive words and phrases she'd already said in one voice or the other. Juggling two personalities was like living with an evil twin. It was only a matter of time until she stumbled. And then what would he do?

This time, she made sure she spoke crisply and lightly, without a hint of the femme fatale. "I find it very hard to believe that the high and mighty Prince of Takeovers is here in my office, telling me he's sorry. You're going to ruin your reputation, you know."

"Why is everyone so concerned about my reputation all of a sudden?"

"Who else?"

"It doesn't bear repeating," he murmured.

His attitude told her the answer, even if he was too polite. "Oh, I get it. Karla. She told you that hanging around with me is going to destroy your good name."

"No. Other way around." His gaze grew warmer. "If I hang around, I'll be destroying *your* good name. I don't care. Do you?"

"Don't make me laugh." But she did, anyway.

"Well, if she knew the whole story, I'm sure she'd feel that way," he declared. "As it happens, I grew up with a single mother, too. My father died when I was very young. I got a stepfather when I was ten, and he's really a nice guy, but he's also a plumber. So I'm probably just as déclassé as you are in their eyes."

She tipped her head to one side, digesting this new information. Funny, but she'd never imagined that anyone as self-possessed and all-around spectacular as Rowan could've grown up without all of life's advantages. "I never thought... I mean..." She hesitated. "I'm surprised, that's all. I guess we all feel our own situation is unique."

"And it is. My single mother was different from your single mother." His mouth quirked into a grin. "And thank God, there were no Farleys in Flatbush."

"Lucky you."

"Lucky me."

They just sat there, smiling at each other, as C.J. mused on the fact that he had found out what she'd hoped he would never learn. And it hadn't worked out badly at all. In fact, she liked him even better now that she'd seen his reaction to her less-than-stellar beginnings.

Maybe he would understand about Buzz and the revenge plan, too, if she could just get up enough gumption to tell him...

But she stopped herself before she thought it. No, he wouldn't understand. And she wasn't going to tell him. Illegitimacy was one thing. A life devoted to revenge was something different altogether.

But, oh, brother, she wished she could think of a way... Rowan was still petting the cat, who was purring so loudly that C.J. could hear it all the way across the room. She was glad the cat liked him so well, but was jealous, too. His hands had caressed her like that yesterday, while she was Cinderella.

And when his fingers had cupped her breast, scorching her through her thin camisole, the little moans of pleasure she'd made weren't so different from Samantha's eager purrs and trills.

C.J.'s face flamed, and she picked up a brochure off her desk to fan herself frantically. She had to get her mind off yesterday; she had to forget his hands and his mouth and the hot, desperate look in his eyes.

"Are you all right? You look a little flushed," he said with concern, and he rose from the chair, setting Samantha off to one side.

"No, no, I'm fine." She opened the brochure, pretending to be very engrossed in reading it. "It's just a little warm in here."

"Actually it feels fine to me." He stuck a hand under the peak of her cap, his palm to her forehead, and she closed her eyes, trying not to melt into a puddle on the floor. "You do feel hot. Are you sure you're not running a fever?"

But of course she was. She had a bad case of the Rowan McKenna flu. "Maybe I am," she returned. She pulled back, spinning away in her chair, away from his hands and his eyes, fanning herself harder. "Running a fever, I mean."

"Can I take a look at that?" He plucked the folded advertisement from her nerveless fingers. "I really am serious about having you build me a barn, and I'd like to get it going as soon as possible."

"Actually I don't build them," she said, automatically falling into her well-worn spiel. It was a good excuse not to look at him, anyway. "I only renovate or restore existing structures."

He leaned in a bit closer, trying to catch her eyes with his rapt, intense gaze. "Will you do one for me?"

At that moment, she would've done absolutely anything for him, short of jumping off the Empire State Building. But why nitpick? If the Empire State Building presented itself, she would've done that, too.

"Are you really going to be around long enough to use it?" she asked wistfully.

"Yes, I am." He grinned at her. "And maybe I'll bring my mom and my little sisters out, too. Maybe Elspeth and Ivy will be best friends."

"Elspeth?" she asked. "Is your mother named Elspeth?"

He sat back. "What's so funny about that?"

"Nothing," she assured him. But she knew she was smiling. "You just don't look like the child of an Elspeth, that's all."

"I am." He held up a few fingers. "Scout's honor."

"Okay, okay, I believe you." She knew she looked like a misty fool, staring up at him, trying not to drool over his classic jaw and his firm, clever mouth. If she could just find a handy phone booth and turn back into Cinderella, she could do whatever her heart desired with this man. He was hers for the taking.

But that was the rub.

She wasn't Cinderella now. She was plain old C.J. And that just wasn't good enough.

She busied herself with the calendar on her desk, flipping pages and pretending to assess her schedule. "I'm pretty busy right now. And it will take some time to find something in the right condition to start with.

Can I get back to you on this?" At least stalling him would give her time to regain her sanity. She hoped.

"Sure." But he made no move to leave.

"Was there something else?"

"Well..." He propped his long, lean body up against her filing cabinet. Lucky filing cabinet. "Now that I'm here, I was wondering if you help me with something."

"Me?" She couldn't imagine Rowan needing her help with absolutely anything.

"It's about a woman."

Oh, no. He's going to ask me about myself again.

"The woman in the picture—the one I showed you at Odell's office."

"The beautiful one you're moving heaven and earth to find," she finished for him. Where was this leading?

"Right."

All innocence, she asked, "Did you find her?"

"In a way. I guess you could say I found her, and then lost her again."

"Oh, dear. Well, I'm sorry. I guess. I mean, if you're sorry you lost her. Again." *Good grief.* She was terrible at this lying and covering-up stuff. She got up and fiddled with the stack of mail in her In basket. "But I thought you weren't going to talk to me about her. Didn't we come to that conclusion back at the picnic?"

She hoped she had a handle on the right conversation. She distinctly remembered getting very angry that he thought he was in love with a ghost and stomping off. She was herself then, wasn't she?

"I know, and I'm sorry. But I'm going crazy," he said tersely. "This is driving me so nuts I can't see straight."

How was she supposed to respond to that? Should she tell him to forget about her, when she thought she would die if he did? Or tell him not to give up, when she was already sick to death of that awful alter ego?

Her brain on overload, C.J. said nothing, just let him go on with his sorry tale about the beautiful, sexy, fabulous woman he was so besotted by. She wanted to kill him.

"I'm sorry, but I don't see how I can help you with someone who sounds like she needs psychiatric help," she interjected. "Showing up, running off... Making herself this mystery woman. She sounds like a lunatic."

She was talking about herself, but she knew the accusation was warranted. She *did* need her head examined!

"I'm really sorry to bring this to you, but, Clementine, I don't know what I think anymore." He jammed his hands in his pockets. "I came here ready to tell you that I am definitely, absolutely, one hundred percent in love with her, but—"

She couldn't stand another minute of this. "Rowan, I really find this a little too personal. Could you please—"

"But then when I'm not with her, I start to think..." He broke off, giving her the strangest look. "I can't be this indecisive. I'm not like that. Everybody who knows me will tell you—I decide I want something, and that's it. I go for it, and I get it. Nothing stands in my way."

"I believe you," she swore. "Really."

He slammed a fist down on her desk, making her jump back. "Then why can't I make up my mind?"

"I thought you already had."

"But that's just it. When I'm with her, I'm sure. But then she vanishes again. And as soon as she's out of my sight..."

"As soon as she's out of your sight, what?"

"I have serious doubts," he said grimly. "And not knowing when or if she'll turn up again is making me berserk. I mean, if I knew for sure she wasn't coming back, then I could make certain decisions that need to be made. But if, on the other hand, she is coming back, then I don't really think it's fair not to wait for her. Do you see what I mean?"

"Not even close."

But he was on a roll. "So this is what I have to know." He gave her the full benefit of that heart-stopping gaze. "After everything I've told you, do you think she'll come back again?"

"I have no idea," she said quickly.

"Come on—just give me your best guess. If it were you, and you had really found a connection with someone, with a stranger, would you let that go? Or would you try again?"

Unfortunately, she knew the answer to this question. She would've tried to evade, but she couldn't break their interlocked gazes. Cautiously she asked, "Did she say she would come back?"

"Yes," he told her.

"And do you think she's a woman of her word?"

"I don't know." He ran a rough hand through his hair. "No, that's not true. I do know. Yes, she's a woman of her word. She has such an honesty about her, even though I know she's keeping back so much. But still, I know she wouldn't lie."

She felt a warm glow at his words. As unhappy as she'd made him, he still trusted her! Or at least he trusted the mysterious Cinderella part of her split personality. But that meant he felt more for her than just some lusty attraction to an artificially pretty face. Didn't it?

As simply as she knew how, she said, "If she said she would, and you believe her, then she'll be back, won't she?"

"God, I hope so," he said fervently, and her heart felt as if someone were squeezing it in two.

The bereft expression on his face, the pain in his voice, made her want to wrap her arms around him and take all the nasty stuff far, far away. At that moment, she was so very sorry for what she'd done. But how could she fix it?

"Clementine," he said softly, and she looked up, still feeling guilty. He gave her a crooked smile. "Thanks for the advice. Thanks for listening."

First an unlikely friendship with a teenage Miss Firecracker candidate, and now Dear Abby sessions with America's most eligible bachelor. What was her life turning into?

She knew she probably looked like a lovesick fool, but she smiled back at Rowan. "No charge."

"I know you're busy, so I won't keep you." Before she could reach out to stop him, to say any of the silly and dangerous things hovering there at the tip of her tongue, Rowan reached for her, brushing his lips across her cheek. "Thanks again," he said gruffly. And then he backed up quickly, moving for the door.

"Wait!" she called.

He turned. "What is it?"

Her heart was pounding so hard that she could barely hear herself think. *I'm the woman you want, the woman you need. Please look at me and see who I am.*

He looked at her, all right. As he paused there, his gaze was dark and intense. She could almost believe he heard her.

"It *is* hot in here," he whispered. His hand was on the doorknob. "I have to—"

"Rowan, I need to know where you live."

"Where I live?"

I need to know where you live so I can make the visit I promised. But she improvised quickly, holding up her datebook. "When I decide, about the barn, I'll need to know where to contact you."

"Oh, right."

And he fired off the address of a luxurious, postmodern house in the woods on the other side of town. She knew the place, and knew the upscale couple who owned it and rented it to summer vacationers. Private and grand, surrounded by trees, it was a perfect setting for upscale, postmodern Rowan. It was also a perfect setting for her date with destiny, her promised visit to see him one more time.

Would she really be so foolish as to challenge the lion in his own den?

Yes, she would.

He had a very strange look on his face as he pushed out the door. "Keep in touch," he told her.

She couldn't hold back a mysterious smile. "Oh, I will. I promise you that."

IT HAD HAPPENED AGAIN.

He was crazy. He'd been lucky to make it out the door, what with all the sultry, sexy looks C.J. was sending him. And he wanted to send them back! He was about as constant as a shifting sand dune.

"Oh, God," he whispered, turning the key in the ignition, but not bothering to put the car in gear. He was too confused to drive at the moment.

After seeing his Cinderella, he had felt so sure she was the right one. He'd had it all neatly tied up in his mind, with one woman as the answer to his dreams, and the other nothing more than a friend.

With his mind made up, he had decided to go see C.J. A bad move, but he'd felt bad about pressuring her about her mother, and he had also wanted to clear the air between them, to make sure they both knew where they stood. So he'd barged in there, all prepared to say something old and hackneyed like It's the best thing for both of us if we're just friends.

So why had he taken one look at her and completely forgotten about the woman in white, who was supposed to be his one true love?

And then he'd blurted out all that nonsense about the other woman, trying to be honest, trying to let her know how conflicted he was.

But C.J. had told him to wait for Cinderella.

He didn't understand. If she thought he should wait for his dream woman, then why did she look at him that way? Why did she jump when he touched her?

Why did she make him want her as much as he wanted his beautiful Cinderella?

Someone on the car radio began to sing, "Love the one you're with," and Rowan didn't know whether to laugh or cry.

Chapter Ten

"Clementine, I must voice my sternest disapproval," Miss Pru said, as the grandfather clock behind her struck midnight. Her normally soft gray eyes shone with distress. "My dear, this is very dangerous. In his current state, that young man is capable of nearly anything!"

C.J. shivered, contemplating exactly what those strong arms and clever hands, and that big, bad body were capable of. She shivered again. Visiting him so late at night, trekking all alone onto his turf, was more than dangerous; it was downright stupid. But she had wrestled with her conscience all day yesterday, all night last night, and all day again today. There was simply no other answer. She had to go.

"I appreciate your concern, but I promised, Miss Pru. I gave my word."

"Yes, I realize that, but—"

"I'll be fine," she assured Miss Pru. "I can handle Rowan."

Her elderly friend's rosebud mouth pursed with disapproval. "You haven't handled him very well so far, have you?" she asked tartly.

"Well, no, but..." She glanced up. She hadn't told Miss Pru any of the details of the disastrous meeting at the park, so how did she know? "What do you mean?"

"I mean the picnic, young lady. You came back with your dress, or perhaps I should call it what it is and say your *undergarments*, all rumpled and mussed. I have eyes, my dear." Miss Pru softened. "It seemed to me you were not exercising the best control over the situation."

"I know. You're absolutely right." C.J. leaned in closer to the old cheval mirror as she applied a new lipstick she'd borrowed from Rainy Day's treasure trove of beauty-pageant supplies. "But Rowan has had all sorts of hints, and he hasn't picked up on a thing."

The lipstick, called "Positively Peachy," looked great on her, and it was only part of the whole palette her new teenage pal had picked out for her. Unfortunately most of the eye stuff was for brown eyes, not violet, but she could hardly explain why she would need purple shadows and liners for those occasions when her eyes changed color.

Eager to be of service, Rainy Day had even found the outfit C.J. was wearing tonight—a simple white halter dress that had been hanging in the back of Petticoat Junction, waiting for someone who never came back to get it off layaway. Although now there was yet another witness to this ongoing saga of deception, C.J. hadn't said a word about where she was going in the dress, and she figured she was okay as long as Rowan didn't have a chance to describe it to Rainy Day, and no one else saw her in it.

Whew. Life had become a morass of deception and cover-up.

"Now you're not even bothering to cover up your identity," Miss Pru added. "No mask, no dark glasses... My dear, this is very foolhardy."

"I honestly don't think he's ever going to get it," she returned. "For goodness' sake, he came to *me* asking for advice about *her!*"

"Oh, dear."

"I know. It's pathetic." But she gave her hair a careless toss and then applied another coat of mascara, sort of enjoying this new glamour-girl look. "How bizarre," she murmured to her reflection. "I'm actually getting good at this."

"You may be attaining expert status, but it still isn't you," Miss Pru sniffed. "I preferred the old Clementine, the one in the dungarees, the one with the lovely, natural hazel eyes and none of that goo on her face."

With an eye pencil dangling in her hand, C.J. turned to look at her friend. "I know," she said softly. "I preferred her, too. But unfortunately Rowan doesn't look twice at her. He doesn't even see her."

"Then he is a very shortsighted young man."

"Shortsighted he may be, but he's not any different from any other man. Appearance is what counts to all of them," she muttered, going back to her task.

"I refuse to believe it," Miss Pru said stoutly.

"It's true. And you know it is." She smiled fondly at the woman who had filled in as her fairy godmother from the beginning. "You were the one who started it, you know, with the evening dress and the diamond earrings and the perfume. Not to mention spending two hours with the curling iron making my hair behave. Turning the sow's ear into a silk purse was all your idea."

"Pish posh." But she wasn't really disagreeing.

"At first all this stuff was just a disguise," C.J. mused. "But it's gone beyond that, hasn't it? I'm dressing up as someone I'm not because a man likes me better that way." Feeling very unsettled, C.J. dropped the eye liner in the cardboard box with the rest of the makeup. "I'm beginning to think I'm no better than the Farley girls."

"Of course you are." The old lady patted her hand gently. "You're still yourself underneath, and that's what counts."

She glanced down at the woman she had become, in a Marilyn Monroe dress and fake fingernails painted peach to match her lipstick. "I feel like a Ping-Pong ball, bouncing back and forth between my personalities."

"It's when you adopt a third one that you'll know you're in trouble," Miss Pru said helpfully.

"I don't think there's any danger of that." But she gave Miss Pru a plaintive gaze. "Am I doing the right thing?"

"Clementine, my dear, you're the only one who knows the answer to that question. But it's not too late to change your mind, especially considering the hour."

It was very late, and very dark outside the cozy old house. Did she really want to go venturing into a lion's den with "bedtime snack" stamped across her forehead?

Her butterflies were threatening to become something more on the order of baby elephants jumping up and down in her stomach, but she tried to be strong.

After all, she had no choice. Squaring her shoulders, C.J. said bravely, "It's only one night—only a few hours. I can handle it. I promised."

She wondered whether Miss Pru saw through the flimsy excuse. Whatever pretense she chose this time— to make sure he didn't print any more pictures, or because she'd given her word, or because he seemed so miserable and she didn't want to be the cause—she knew the real reason she was going.

She wanted to be with him. And nothing was going to stand in her way.

C.J. KNEW THE WAY to the house he was leasing. But it was a very dark night, and she took a few wrong turns, meaning she was even later than she'd expected to be when she finally got there.

She couldn't very well call to announce she was coming, but maybe she could've figured out some way to drop him a hint. This way, arriving unannounced, she was taking her chances.

What if he was asleep, and she woke him up, still tousled and warm from the bed? She fanned her quickly overheating imagination.

Okay, what if she interrupted an assignation with some other woman? That one was easier. "I'll kill him," she said out loud, switching off her lights and looking for a good place to stow her truck. "I'll kill him, and I'll throw her in the woods."

Proceeding carefully she hid the truck off to the side of a small, isolated gravel road, and then hoofed it around the bend to his house. The whole trip was reminiscent of that fateful night at the country club, but at least this time she was wearing flat sandals, which were a heck of a lot easier to walk in.

A ghostly glow beckoned to her from his house, with a few rays of light glimmering through the tall, dark trees, telling her Rowan was either still up or slept with the lights on. She tried to move quietly but steadily in the right direction, heading toward those lights. But her heart was pounding and her ears were ringing, and it only got worse the closer she came to his house. By the time her foot touched the flagstones out front, her heartbeat was so fast and so erratic that she thought she might faint.

She opened her mouth wider, taking in full, deep gulps of the hot, sticky air. The brisk walk in such muggy weather had made her drip with sweat, and she raised a hand to wipe her brow, hoping her hair and her makeup had survived. She had no experience with these kinds of things. A trickle of perspiration slid down between her breasts, but there was nothing she could do about that. If she'd wanted to arrive crisp and collected for her last appearance as Cinderella, she had not gotten her wish.

Nonetheless, here she was, signed, sealed and delivered. Now what? Did she ring the bell? Or would he automatically turn on all the lights and expose her to the glare of reality if he came to open the door?

Should she break in and risk Dobermans and burglar alarms?

Or should she turn tail and run back home the way she wanted to?

As C.J. stood there, contemplating her fate, she could hear the jagged edge of her own heartbeat, loud against a backdrop of buzzes and hums in the sultry, still night. The buzzing came from crickets in the woods that surrounded the house, but the hum she couldn't identify.

She could smell the dark, shadowy night, the piney trees and the cedar shakes on the house, mingled with the faint scent of her own perfume. It was, all in all, a very heady mixture.

The whole front of the house was dark, and she saw now that the lights she'd spotted from the road must be around the back, on the deck. She remembered the house fairly well; she'd helped the owners find just the right wood trim for their staircase, and just the right whirlpool spa for their deck. It was really a very striking place, with lots of glass and open spaces inside. It also featured an opulent multilevel deck that the owners always used as a selling point when it came time to rent it for the summer.

Everybody loved that deck. And unless she missed her guess, the current occupant was using it right now.

The hum she'd heard before had to be the whirlpool in action. Unless he left his spa running without him, Rowan McKenna was on that deck, in that spa, soaking his muscles and steaming his naked skin.

C.J. began to tremble. *Hold on,* she told herself. *You don't know he's naked.*

But she had a very good idea.

Before she had a chance to remind herself what a fool she was, she slid around the side of the house, skirting the trees as she made her way slowly but surely toward the back. She saw the lights again before she saw him. They were small Japanese lanterns, strung lazily around the outside of the deck, offering a dim glow and shining softly on the back of his dark head.

From her angle, she could see that he was submerged in the bubbling water up to his chest, with his head tilted back and his eyes closed. His bare, beautifully muscled arms gripped the outside apron of the sunken tub, and he had a tumbler in one hand, half filled with amber liquid.

She saw a portable bar of some sort over by the far edge of the deck, but no towel or robe anywhere. If he was nude, he wasn't planning on covering up anytime soon. The night was already hot enough, but suddenly it felt suffocating.

Completely out of the blue, he stood up. He looked like a Greek god rising from the surf, with lucky little rivulets licking him all the way up and down, and she gasped. She had to bite her lip to keep from crying out at the sheer perfection of the view.

"Who's there?" he demanded.

She panicked. She tried to turn and run the other direction, but all she succeeded in doing was tripping over the cord to the lights. As she steadied herself, the lanterns careened wildly, casting crazy, wicked shadows all over the deck.

"Who's there?" he asked again, with a surlier edge this time.

C.J. knew she had to identify herself, or risk his naked body flying off the deck and tackling her in the grass. "It's me," she whispered, hiding behind a bush.

"Who?"

She saw she had no other options; she was going to have to face him and his fabulous naked body and try not to embarrass herself. Slowly she climbed a few creaky steps to the first level, wincing at the noise.

"You," he said roughly.

She swallowed. "Yes, it's me."

As she took a few more steps, rising to the second tier, she saw that he had sagged back into the whirlpool. With his gaze blistering a hole into her, he noted, "So you did come."

"I promised, didn't I?"

"How do I know what your promises are worth?"

"You do now." She was only a few feet away now, and she smiled awkwardly, feeling like a wayward schoolgirl standing there in her summery white dress.

She had read before that business sharks boosted their chairs for important meetings, making sure they could look down on their rivals. The higher vantage point was supposed to give them a psychological edge. But C.J. could attest that at this moment, all the advantage was on Rowan's side, even though she loomed five and a half feet above him, even though she was fully clothed and he wasn't wearing a stitch.

He just kept staring at her, and she wondered desperately if her mascara had smudged or her lipstick had gotten stuck to her teeth. Dream lovers were not supposed to have flaws in their appearance, or doubts, either. It was all out of character for any Cinderella worth her salt to be insecure like this, but she couldn't help it.

"Is there something wrong?" she asked.

A long pause hung in the humid air. Finally, just when she was about ready to throw herself into the whirlpool and throttle him, he broke his intense scrutiny. He jiggled the glass in his hand, rattling the ice cubes, as he said, "I've never seen you before, you know. Without one of your masks in between us."

But you still don't see me, do you? It was the moment of truth. He'd seen her whole face, and he still didn't know. She should've felt triumph; there was going to be a big I-told-you-so for Miss Pru. But instead she felt disappointed one more time.

"I promised that, too," she murmured. "Don't you remember? No masks, no dark glasses. I gave my word."

"So you did." Rowan took a long swallow from his drink. "Thank you." He looked up swiftly, catching her by surprise, but his words were cold. "You're as beautiful as I knew you'd be. As beautiful and as perfect and as distant."

This wasn't working out how she'd planned at all. He seemed to be in a very foul mood, and her presence was only making it worse.

"In his current state, that young man is capable of nearly anything," Miss Pru had said. What if she was right?

He jiggled his glass again. "Oh, I'm sorry. Where are my manners?"

She wanted to remind him that he didn't seem to have any when he was around this half of her personality, what with hauling her into his arms every time she showed up, but she refrained.

"Would you like a drink?" he asked gallantly. "I'd get up, but I'm in no condition."

Her cheeks flamed. Surely he didn't mean... Or maybe he did.

"There's Scotch," he went on, "and an ice bucket over there, on that cart by the bench."

Normally she didn't touch Scotch or anything else stronger than a little wine, but tonight she needed the fortification. Quickly she crossed to the liquor cart and poured herself a stiff drink. She choked as she took the first gulp, but at least the burning sensation took her mind off Rowan.

And still he sat there in that damned pool, staring at her, watching her every move.

"Look," she said abruptly. "I don't think I can do this."

"Do what?"

"This. This fencing thing, with you. You're the one who wanted me to come here, and you made me swear I would. So here I am, as promised." She tossed back another belt, a bigger one this time. "But if you don't want me here, if you want to play games with me, then I'm leaving." She gave him a good, strong pause to emphasize her determination. "It's your call. What will it be?"

"I want you to stay," he said immediately.

"But why?" She edged back his direction, returning his malevolent stare. "Why?"

"Because I'm in love with you."

It stung. It stung so bitterly she couldn't breathe for a few seconds. He really thought he'd fallen for a woman he didn't even know?

"You can't be," she said softly.

"And if I am?"

God, he had gorgeous eyes. Even when he was being sullen and moody, his eyes shone with that stunning crystal blue light, and she wanted to fall right in and believe every ridiculous word that fell from his lips.

He sat up straighter, and she had to concentrate hard not to look down into the bubbling, boiling water. His hand rose from the side of the small pool, as if reaching for her. "Sit down beside me," he said. "I want to talk to you."

"No, I—" she tried.

"Come on," he coaxed. "The water feels wonderful. Right now, you have me at a disadvantage. You can keep eluding me, but I'm stuck."

Well, he had a point. She supposed he could've stalked around the deck completely nude, and she honestly wouldn't have put it past him, but she certainly preferred he stay where he was.

"I could go into the house and get you a towel or something," she offered.

"I don't need a towel. I need you to sit down here, with me."

Instead of the brooding act, he was trying sweetness and warmth, it seemed. Once again, she didn't know how to read him.

Slowly she stripped off her sandals and lowered herself to the wooden floor, venturing far enough over to dip her toes in the water. It was very hot, and churning up all sorts of trouble, just like the man occupying the center of the pool.

Actually it did feel good, energizing and relaxing her feet and her calves. She'd been standing most of the day, first out at a construction site and then finishing Rainy Day Delmar's beauty-pageant props, so she was a bit tired. Pushing her dress an inch or so above her knees, she slid farther into the water, until she was hovering on the edge.

"Oooh," she whispered. "That feels great."

It did feel great, as far as it went. Too bad the rest of her was still so sweaty and sticky.

"Why not come in the rest of the way?"

Was he the devil himself, or did he just sound that way? She cast a suspicious eye at Rowan, who had gotten a whole lot closer within the past few seconds. When he smiled lazily, both he and the water looked very inviting.

"I don't have a bathing suit," she pointed out.

"Neither do I."

"I noticed."

"I know."

There was a short pause. "I guess you win that round," she said breathlessly.

"Are you coming in?"

"I don't think so—" she began, but then his strong arms were lifting her into the pool before she could get the words out.

It wasn't deep, but deep enough. As she splashed down into the bubbles, her white dress plastered itself to her body, and Rowan quickly pulled her over onto his lap.

But it was too late. She'd already seen what she looked like. As the water cascaded over her breasts, outlining every inch of her, her nipples were peaking, forming small, rosy circles that showed right through the front of her dress. She might as well have been stripped bare for all the cover she was getting from her clothes.

And they both knew it.

"Don't worry about it," he whispered, and his breath puffed warm into her ear, as one hard arm slipped around behind her.

"Oh, this isn't smart," she whispered, but it was much too late for that.

She was here. He was here. And they were both getting what they wanted.

His mouth descended on hers, and she wrapped her arms around his neck as if there was no tomorrow. As far as she was concerned, there wasn't.

He tasted like Scotch, and so did she. Their mouths together tasted like heaven. She couldn't get enough of the way he felt, with his skin so slick and steamy from the whirlpool. Her hands glided over his strong shoulders, enjoying the interplay of muscle and bone that made him so different from her, as he edged her around to meet his mouth more fully.

Her skirt was floating somewhere around her waist, and she slapped it out of the way, turning into him, kissing him back and pressing herself closer. Without quite realizing what she was doing, just trying to brace herself, she found herself straddling his lap, with only her thin panties in between her and the very obvious evidence of his desire.

She tried to move, but only succeeded in rubbing against him. When he groaned, she shot backward, saying raggedly, "I'm sorry. I didn't mean—"

But he smiled and pulled her back where she'd been, murmuring soft words, nibbling her neck and her earlobe, sliding her knees alongside his hips, until she was settled there very securely. Hungrily he slid his hands up her thighs to the curve of her bottom, cupping her buttocks, urging her even nearer.

She had never been this close to a man, so close that she had no idea where his flesh ended and hers began. Around them, the water was seething and foaming, but it was nothing compared to the storm of passion raging inside her. Her whole body was tingling and throbbing, as Rowan held her and touched her and drove her out of her mind. And then he stripped off her panties and tossed them away, bringing them skin to skin.

It felt wonderful, and she angled herself in closer, harder, loving the feel of him beneath her, loving the wild little sounds he made when she wiggled like that, loving the sense of power she got from turning up his temperature controls.

"Oh, yes," she whispered. "Oh, yes."

But he didn't offer release, not yet. He tilted her back, still inside the hard circle of his arms. And then he bent his head to her breast, laving and tugging at the wet cloth and her hard little nipples underneath, while ribbons of desire tied and untied her.

But she wanted to feel his mouth on her skin, without the impediment of the dress. "Take it away," she said unsteadily, untying the top of her halter and trying to peel away the unwanted dress.

He smiled and kissed her again, nudging her hands aside, leaving the dress pooled at her waist. And then he just looked at her for a long moment, and his voice was uneven when he said, "I've seen this picture in my head for a long time. But it didn't compare to the real thing."

Greedily he moved his hand over one bare breast, and lowered his lips to the tip of the other. She moaned and cried out, clenching her fists in his hair and holding him fast.

Still, she shivered with restless desire, until finally he reached for her dress. With one swift motion, he disposed of it, leaving her as naked and as ready as he was.

She could see the perspiration on his forehead, and the glazed, ravenous look in his eyes, as he stopped, holding back for one second and then two. "Are you sure?" he asked.

And she nodded.

After one quick kiss and then another, he held her tight in his embrace, easing her down and thrusting up at the same time, telling her how good it felt as he sheathed himself inside her.

She thought she would die of bliss. Incoherent, trembling with need, she licked his neck and bit his ear and clutched his strong shoulders, as he stroked and moved, lifting her, claiming her, tossing her higher and higher until she cried out, "Now, Rowan, now."

And with one last surge, one tiny touch, they fell over the pinnacle . . . together.

They lay there in the whirlpool for a long moment, as the water eddied and swirled around them, as Rowan rocked her in his arms, smoothing her hair away from her face, brushing his cheek against hers.

"I do love you," he whispered. "You can deny it all you want, but the feelings are there between us. It wouldn't feel like this if I didn't love you. It wouldn't feel like this if you didn't love me."

She shook her head. "I can't love you."

"You do."

"I won't love you."

"You don't have a choice."

"There is a problem," she put in, trying to be sensible.

How about a whole mountainload of them? Starting with the fact that she had deceived him from the word go, and ending with the fact that she had plenty of plans on her plate without adding him to the mix.

She had held on to revenge against Buzz Farley as the single most important thing in her life for so long that she didn't know who she would be without it.

Yet how did a person go about telling her brand-new lover that she had been engaging in, and had every intention of continuing to engage in, some very questionable activities in order to financially ruin the man who was her unacknowledged, illegitimate father? Her body was still warm from his love, and her head was spinning with obstacles.

"I can fix problems," he told her, dropping hungry kisses on her chin and her neck. "You tell me what it is, and I'll make it go away."

"I don't need you to fix it." She covered his mouth with hers quickly, to shut him up. "I need *me* to fix it."

"But I can help," he insisted.

"Yes, you can." C.J. found a bright smile and flashed it at him. "You can help by getting me a robe or something to wear for the rest of the night."

His own grin was so adorable that it would've knocked her socks off if she'd been wearing any. "You'll stay the night?"

"I would love to," she said lightly, lying through her teeth.

He gave her a sweet, clinging kiss that made her very sorry for what she was about to do. It made her want to forget all about Buzz Farley and the whole lousy scheme and make a dozen babies with Rowan McKenna.

But as soon as his terrific little bottom cleared the sliding glass doors into the house, C.J. grabbed her dress and her shoes and headed for the hills. She struggled into the wet, impossible clothes as she ran, not walked, across the lawn and down the road.

Behind her, she heard no commotion, no uproar, to indicate he was coming after her. Her heart contracted with the pain she'd just inflicted.

But, no, he wouldn't follow. Not this time. How many times could she run out on the same man before he washed his hands of her?

And after what they'd shared... This was one exit he would never be able to forgive.

Jumping into the truck, she hazarded a glance in the rearview mirror and immediately wished she hadn't. All of her makeup had washed off hours ago, and her hair was so wet that it no longer held even a hint of curl. Her disguise was in tatters, as limp as the soggy halter dress she'd worn in the pool.

It didn't occur to her until she was five miles down the road that she had not remembered, not even once, to use the special husky voice she'd made up for Cinderella.

All night, she'd been speaking in her normal voice. And he had heard every word.

Chapter Eleven

Rowan wasn't worried. He'd told himself that ten times in the past half hour, so he said it again just for good measure. He wasn't worried.

She would show up again. Soon. He was sure of it.

This time, he knew what he felt, and he was arrogant enough to think he knew what *she* felt, too. Okay, so she'd decided to disappear again. Annoying, yes, but hardly an indictment. And he had certainly been aware she was capable of it.

"No," he said, jamming his hand in his pocket to get a reassuring touch of his old friend, the bottle rocket. "No, I'm not worried."

"Mr. McKenna!" called out a plump, middle-aged blonde whose name he had forgotten. She plucked at his jacket sleeve, pulling him along to a table set up in about the middle of the high school auditorium. "You sit over here at the judges' table, right next to where Karla and Darla Farley will be when they arrive."

His least favorite people ... He thought of walking out right then, but that wouldn't have been fair. After all, somebody had to judge the poor contestants, and they shouldn't be left to the likes of the Farley girls.

The blonde glanced nervously at her watch. "Those Farleys should've been here by now. Vesta!" she shouted. "Have you seen Karla and Darla?" Not getting any answer, she trilled, "Well, here's another fire for me to stamp out. You sit down, Mr. McKenna, and *don't move!*"

Although he thought it was awfully sporting of him, he obliged, edging his chair as far to one side of the table as it would go. After he'd hung out in Sparks this long, it was beginning to seem strange to wear a suit and tie, but he'd donned some of his natty New York attire for his job as a beauty-pageant judge. In honor of the young Miss Firecracker candidates, Rowan had worn tan pleated trousers with a dark green jacket, a white shirt and a tie that looked as if it had big marbles on it. It was definitely not a Sparks look.

He knew it was nuts, but he figured he'd at least look nice if he happened to run into the woman he loved.

Last night, he thought. *Only last night I had her in my arms.* So why did it feel as if it had been so long?

He pounded a fist into the flimsy judges' table, flipping a pencil in the air and making everyone seated in the row in front of him jump in surprise. But he was feeling very frustrated, no matter how many times he told himself not to worry. Where was she? And why did she keep running out on him?

And then he saw her.

It hit him in the gut like a cannon blast. She was standing on the other side of the high school auditorium, way down by the stage, fussing with something that looked like a flat cutout of a pig. She was wearing jeans and a work shirt, just as she always did.

She was C. J. Bede.

His mouth fell open, and he had to remind himself to close it. Of course it was C.J. It was so obvious. How could he have failed to see what was right before his eyes?

"Wait a minute," he said. C.J. had hazel eyes, but his mystery woman had those fabulous violet ones.

Contact lenses, he realized. With contacts, different clothes, makeup, maybe some fancy fingernails . . . She had duped him completely.

He was stunned. He was frozen. He was rooted to his seat, unable to move, unable to think, unable to do anything but mumble, "I can't believe it."

There she was, as she always was, running around Sparks, scowling at people. She looked nothing like his Woman in White. And yet, she looked everything like her.

At that moment, if she'd been within arms' reach, he honestly thought he would've killed her. He had agonized about falling for two women at the same time, about being enough of a cad to keep two of them on a string. He had blamed himself!

When all along there was only one.

"I'm going to kill her," he promised himself. If only for the sheer satisfaction of wringing her neck with his bare hands.

A teenage blonde wearing far too much makeup sneaked out from behind the curtain to talk to C.J. They both seemed to be jittery and nervous as C.J. showed her the pig, gesticulating about something that was up behind the curtains. Their conversation furnished plenty of time for Rowan to study her, to look her up, down and sideways.

The way she moved, the way she smiled, the way she tipped her head to one side when she was listening . . . How could he not have noticed? How could he have been so incredibly blind?

He felt like finding a handy brick wall to bash his head against, until he knocked some sense into his thick skull.

When she laughed at something the girl said, his gaze whipped back to her. It was *her* laugh, tickling him, teasing him, mocking him.

That was unquestionably *her* round little bottom, filling out those worn blue jeans.

And those were *her* hands, gesturing in the air. He remembered those small hands clutching him, stroking him . . .

Rowan half rose in his chair, fully intending to vault out of his seat, hurtle over ten rows of people, grab her and shake her till her teeth rattled.

What kind of a game was she playing?

But he stopped. Clenching his jaw, he sat back down. He couldn't, wouldn't hash it out here, in front of all these people. He felt like enough of a fool without sharing it with the greater population of Sparks.

In the pit of his stomach, he suddenly had the horrible idea that this was all a big joke, designed to make him look like an idiot.

But he rejected that idea summarily. Not C.J. It wasn't her style. He knew people. He knew *her*. She wouldn't have done that.

As he sat there in a daze, trying to make some sense of this revelation, more pageant spectators had begun to file into the hall. In fact, now that he looked around, he saw that almost all the seats were filled.

Even his fellow judges, the Farley sisters, had arrived, although they were over at the other end of the table, doing their best to ignore him.

"Thank goodness," he muttered. They were jabbering down there, but Rowan did his best to tune them out. It wasn't hard. He was still sitting there with his mouth hanging open, staring at C.J., acting as if he were a compass and she were due north.

The really awful part was how much he still wanted her. With every breath he took, with every beat of his heart, and especially with every tinkling laugh coming from her beautiful mouth, he wanted her. He wanted her so badly his hands were shaking.

Once again, he pushed back his chair and started to stand.

"Is something wrong?" the blonde in charge asked icily, crossing her arms over her powder pink suit.

"No," he returned. "Why?"

But she just stood there, right next to him, glaring at him, as if she expected him to bolt at any moment, and she would personally bring him down.

He held up his hands in surrender, sitting back in his folding chair, prepared to at least pretend to do his duty by the pageant even if it killed him.

He could wait. He was a patient man.

Now that he knew who she was, he had all the time in the world. And maybe it was better this way. Maybe it was better if he had a little time to let this settle before he did something stupid, like kiss her or throttle her, or both.

Finally the lights dimmed, C.J. disappeared behind the curtains, the three-piece combo passing for an orchestra tuned up on "You Are So Beautiful (to Me)" and the emcee came out to get things started. But Rowan let it pass him by.

As the pageant and its contestants trundled along, Rowan's brain was on overload. He was fighting his way through what he knew, trying to make it add up.

It didn't. Clementine Jemima Bede was his mystery woman, and it made no sense. In fact, he was more baffled than ever. Why the masquerade in the first place? And once she'd done it, why keep it up? Why hadn't she just told him who she was a long time ago?

C.J. was nothing if not honest and forthright, a real straight shooter. Yet she'd been lying to him from the very beginning. Why?

Okay, so he had been enough of a jerk not to recognize her when he saw her again the first time after the ball. He was sure she hadn't taken it as a compliment when he ran out in front of her truck and flagged her down, and then proceeded to ask if she'd seen his Cinderella.

Hell and damnation. She *was* his Cinderella.

He groaned at his own stupidity. No, she wouldn't have been pleased. But still, he didn't understand. He loved her. And now that he knew who she really was, he was even more sure that she wouldn't have come to him last night, she wouldn't have shared that steamy encounter in the whirlpool, if she didn't love him, too.

It was an encouraging thought. "She does love me," he said out loud, earning himself a curious look from Darla, who stopped bickering with her sister long enough to say, "Who loves you?"

But the busy-bee blonde frowned and demanded, "Where are your interview scores?"

"My what?"

"Your prepageant interview scores. You didn't turn them in."

Rowan gave her a blank look. "But I didn't do any prepageant interviews. I don't know anything about them."

"Well, don't tell anyone!" the woman whispered. "Here, it's the pink form. Fill it in as you go along, with whatever you want."

"But won't the girls know I never interviewed them?"

"They won't care. Just do it!" she ordered.

She had a maniacal look in her eye as she shoved the pink sheet at him, and he knew better than to buck a crazed beauty-pageant organizer.

He had been dreading this stupid farce of a pageant, anyway, but being stuck here when his life had been turned upside down was absolute torture. As the parade of teenagers in swimsuits and high heels continued, he jiggled his official judge's pencil in the air, wondering where C.J. had gotten to. He did a systematic scan of the audience, surveying each face, but she wasn't there.

"Get ready for your swimsuit scores!" snarled the blonde, and he sent her his nastiest glare. She stared right back, tapping the green sheet on the pile in front of him.

Halfheartedly he started filling numbers into the spaces, barely glancing at the grinning girls clomping across the stage. At the very end of the line, he recognized the one who'd been talking to C.J. before they began—she was the same kid who'd bashed him with her purse in the Redux Deluxe office—and he automatically gave her a higher score for being friends with the woman he loved. C.J. might be a coward and a cheat, but she was still his. And he was a very loyal man.

Indulging that kind of partisanship, being completely unfair and biased, at least made him smile. So C.J.'s friend was one Rainy Day Delmar. Good. If he had anything to say about it, Rainy Day was going to win this contest.

After the swimsuit section, after their green forms were ripped out of their hands, they were on to the talent competition. If he'd thought the first part was torture, this was like being eaten alive by fire ants. Except it took longer.

The first girl did an agonizing *pas de deux* with a life-size rag doll attached to her feet, and the second one crocheted a potholder, right there on stage. Unfortunately they were the highlights of the evening.

Finally, just when he was idly wondering how much ammo it would require to take out the whole auditorium with a machine gun, it was Rainy Day Delmar's turn. The lighting changed, casting most of the stage into shadow, as a side of a barn smoothly descended stage left, a large whispery rope concoction with a big spider on it dipped down stage right, and a very familiar stage hand wearing blue jeans rushed out to shove on a couple of bales of hay and that big, flat pig he'd seen before.

Rowan sat up straighter, coming to life for the first time in a long while. C.J. All the time he'd been looking for her, she'd been hiding out backstage, waiting to run on with hay bales.

Well, it was certainly the most elaborate scenery they'd had so far. C.J. disappeared, Rainy Day came on, and he sat back, wanting more of the stage hand and less of the star. The girl launched into a singsong recitation of something to do with a dead spider and its pig friend, and he frowned. Since when where pigs and spiders friends? The whole thing seemed nuts to him, but hey, the scenery was great. He penciled in a ten and turned in his talent scores.

"Am I done now?" he asked, ready to bolt and grab C.J. while he still knew where she was.

His keeper gave him a scandalized look. "Oh, my word, no! We're just adding up to see who makes the semifinals. And then there's evening gown, and then the interviews." She dropped her voice, and said meanly, "You have to do your prepageant interviews, too, and don't forget it."

Rowan grabbed his pencil and his pink sheet, wrote in tens for the whole bunch of them and tossed over the form. And then he sat there and stewed.

As the interminable pageant wore on, he was firming up his plans. With one eye on the stage, he mulled it over. All the way through the semifinals, he was intent on a confrontation as soon as possible. But during the evening-gown competition, he started to have a change of heart.

What if he confronted her, and she told him he was wrong? He could just see C.J. calmly saying, Sorry, it wasn't me. No one in town had recognized her, and they'd all back her up now. C. J. Bede at the Firecracker Ball? What, are you crazy?

And as for C.J. herself, well, she was pretty good at playing it cool. After all, she'd looked at her own picture and then given him advice about herself without batting an eye. Denial was a piece of cake.

Besides, what good would it do to confront her, if she refused to tell him the reason behind it all? It wasn't the thing itself that was making him so crazy, it was *why*. And he knew damn well she would clam up and leave him wondering.

So, by the time the final interviews rolled around, Rowan had decided to take a different tack. He might've acted like a fool during this whole thing, but he was going to stop right now.

The chilly, unemotional Prince of Takeovers was back in control. So, no, he wasn't going to confront her. He was going to sit back and watch her, gloating, knowing he knew, but she didn't know he knew. He was going to drive her crazy.

And then there was part two of his plan. As a businessman, his first rule was to know his enemies. He asked questions, he used investigators, he sniffed and studied and calculated. It occurred to him that he needed to know a bit more about Miss Clementine, and the time to start learning was now.

But the libraries and the newspaper office were closed, and he already knew that nobody in town had much to say about C.J. So where could he look?

What he came up with was unethical and probably illegal, and he was going to do it, anyway.

"I'm going to break into her house," he said out loud.

"What?" the blond contest lady asked.

"Nothing," he muttered.

But it wasn't nothing. It was everything. Once he was inside her domain, he'd not only find conclusive proof of the deception—like one of the white dresses or maybe the violet contact lenses—but maybe he could also find some answers.

But first he had to get inside the place. Right now would be a perfect time, since she was otherwise occupied. Unfortunately he was just as occupied as she was.

As he chafed, more than ready to get this show on the road, the emcee announced that they were down to three finalists—Rainy Day, a girl who'd flown like Peter Pan and a fire-baton twirler. The emcee asked them each something about world peace, they each gave awful answers and Rowan gave Rainy Day first place in a flash.

Things began to move more quickly. Somebody put a crown on Rainy Day's head, the girl burst into tears, Karla slapped Darla and shouted, "I didn't want her! What did you vote for her for?" and Rowan leaped to his feet, immediately looking for C.J.

She was off to the side of the stage, grinning at her winning candidate, but not really a part of things. A bunch of people had congregated around the new Miss Firecracker, who was still wailing away up there, clutching her crown and hugging everybody.

Rowan strode up to the stage, weaving in and out of clumps of contestants and moms and dads, heading for C.J. He didn't know what he was going to say to her, but he knew he had to see her up close just once, now that he knew.

"Hi," he said softly, and he saw her jump, startled, before she turned.

"Oh, hello, Rowan."

It took a very good eye to pick up the signs, but he saw them. He saw the way her hands shook, ever so slightly, and she quickly stuffed them in her jeans pockets. He caught the way she wouldn't quite meet his gaze, and the way her nostrils flared, as if she were having trouble taking in enough air.

How could he have missed it before? Was he really that blind? Or had he simply not been looking?

In his own mind, he knew the truth. The old maxim You only see what you want to see flashed in his mind. That was it, in a nutshell.

He'd fallen under the spell of the fantasy of his beautiful Cinderella. He'd believed that she was ethereal and exotic because he'd wanted to believe it.

Funny. Now that he knew the truth, C.J. and her jeans were every bit as sexy as the siren in the low-cut white dress. Now that he knew the truth, she could've been wearing a clown suit, and his blood would still be boiling, his pulses still pounding.

He smiled wickedly. "Hello, Clementine." Being this close, he couldn't help feeling a quick flash of joy, even though he still itched to smack her. He forced himself to widen his smile, if only to make her wonder what the breezy grin was all about. "Your candidate won," he told her. "Congratulations."

"Oh." C.J. took her hands out of her pockets, wiped them on her thighs and then stuck them away again. "So I guess you saw my scenery. No big deal, but I had fun. And I'm glad she won. She's a sweet girl."

"Uh-huh."

"You were a judge, right?"

"Yes, I was."

"Did you enjoy it?"

"I hated it."

"Oh, well, then..." She chewed her lip and shuffled her feet, clearly ill at ease.

Why doesn't she say something? He had to hold himself rigidly under control so he didn't start shouting. Damn her. He wanted her to start handing over confessions, something like I'm sorry I didn't tell you. I love you, too. I have all along.

He wanted her to offer some explanation, to break her silence and begin to make things better. But she didn't.

He wanted the fact that they had made love to make a difference, to make her give up whatever secret she was holding on to so firmly, and give in to what they could be together. But she wouldn't.

She just stood there, with her honest hazel eyes, keeping her mysteries to herself.

He felt sure now that his decision had been the right one. If he asked her about the masquerade, about her other persona, she would simply refuse to tell him. She'd held out this long. Why would she fold now?

Before he confronted her, before he bit her head off, he had to know why.

"Are you doing anything?" he asked casually.

She glanced up in surprise. "Now, you mean?"

He nodded.

"Well, yes, I am. Rainy Day's mother is having a party for her, to celebrate winning and everything, and Rainy Day insisted I come." She licked her lips. "I suppose you could come, too, if you wanted to."

He was a bit surprised at this turn of events. Was she actually asking him to come along?

"It won't be very exciting, but I do feel I should go," she went on. "Just a bunch of high school kids, and some of the other contestants and their parents—I don't plan to stay very long, but if you wanted to come..."

He didn't have time for sweet little social engagements. He had a house to burgle. *I'm going to make you pay,* he promised her silently. *I'm going to turn you over my knee and paddle your behind...*

He forced himself to glance down at his watch. "Almost midnight," he said casually. "I didn't realize it was so late. I should probably get home."

She nodded. "Well, I'd better go."

"Have fun," he said darkly.

And while she played with the new Miss Firecracker, he planned to go find the answers he needed.

"Just wait, Clementine," he whispered. "Just wait till you see what I've got in store for you."

Chapter Twelve

He had never before in his life broken into anything. But C.J.'s front door wasn't even locked. Did it count as breaking and entering if it wasn't locked?

Oh, the hell with it. C.J. was hardly going to turn him in. Besides, she was off partying with Miss Firecracker, and he had at least a few minutes to look for clues. Her barn of a house was out in the middle of nowhere, so he thought it was safe to turn on a few lights.

"Nice place," he said admiringly, casting an appreciative eye over the soaring beams and golden wood. An Amish quilt hung the length of one wall, while a pair of old snowshoes hung opposite, over the fireplace. All the decorations were breezy and irreverent, with bold splashes of color and a minimum of fuss.

The cat he'd met at her office bolted out from under a chair and came skidding to a stop near his foot. "Hi, there," he said softly, picking her up and letting her lick his hand. But he realized it was idiotic to break into someone's house and start petting their cat. He didn't have that much time to begin with, and he knew he'd better get moving.

Unfortunately he didn't find anything interesting in his methodical search of the first floor, which seemed to be one big room, roughly divided into kitchen and living spaces. It was all interesting, actually, because it gave him a better idea of what made C.J. tick, and maybe what made him tick, too.

He realized he might've been bluffing when he started, but he really did love this barn. He'd seen it in the photo in her office before, but close up was even better. Oddly enough, he could see himself sitting in front of the fire with C.J., popping popcorn, sharing a glass of wine. Or maybe curled up together on the red sofa...

Not until after I kill her, he thought grimly. He forced himself away from the cozy stuff, aimlessly picking up a teapot shaped like a race car, and going through the motions of looking inside it. But the fact that she had a terrific house or a very funky teapot collection hardly told him why she was playing dress-up and haunting his dreams.

Nonetheless, he persevered, taking the open-slatted stairs to the second-floor loft area. A glance at his watch told him it was getting close to one o'clock. He'd already been in the house for almost half an hour, and he hadn't found a thing. He didn't think she'd stay at the pageant party long, given the time, and if he wanted a better look before he had to leave, he'd better get a move on.

So he went ahead into her bedroom, even though it definitely gave him pause. Searching her living room was one thing. Poking around someone's bedroom in the still of night felt a lot creepier somehow.

But he couldn't help a certain curiosity. She wasn't exactly neat, with her bed linens unmade and blue jeans all over the floor, but there was nothing remarkable here, no wisps of lingerie to remind him of their brief encounter in the whirlpool, not even a secret diary to thoughtfully detail whatever it was she was hiding. No, there were still no answers here, and no Cinderella costumes, either.

He began to actually have doubts that it was really C.J. Maybe his eyes had deceived him. Maybe she had a look-alike cousin or sister...

And then he heard the loud sound of an engine, on the highway close by, and he stopped dead in his tracks. Was that C.J.'s truck? He dashed the lights quickly, and then felt his way back out to the stairs.

He could see the cat's eyes glowing down there in the main room, and with that to guide him, he slipped down and out the door in about two seconds. As the lights of C.J.'s pickup came bouncing up the gravel road, Rowan hid behind the trunk of a big, gnarled oak in her yard, waiting for her to park and pass him by.

Whistling something to herself, Clementine shoved her car door shut and started for the house. When she was right next to where he was skulking behind the tree, she hesitated, as if she sensed his presence.

Rowan held his breath and tried to act invisible, and it must have worked. She shrugged and walked on by.

Against his tree, he sagged with relief. As she opened the door, he heard her say, "Hmmm. I left the light on in the kitchen."

"No, I did," he muttered, but he slid out from behind the oak and raced over to the cover of her office, just in case she looked out the window of her house.

Her office was just across the yard from the house, no more than fifty feet away. As he moved past it, crouching like a cat burglar, he stopped suddenly. When he was in the office with C.J., he remembered there had been paper strewn everywhere. Surely those papers would tell him something.

He ventured a quick glance back at the house. If she looked out, she might very well see the lights in the office. Oh, what the hell. He was willing to risk it. After all, she was the one with something to hide.

The door to the office was locked, but it only took a few seconds with a credit card to get it open. Living in New York for all those years had come in handy.

Rowan pushed inside, wincing at the audible creak, and looked around. The first thing he noticed was that sampler over on the wall.

"A woman scorned," he mused. That had to figure into this somehow. He could understand if he'd been the one to break her mother's heart, and she was making a fool of him in revenge, but that clearly wasn't it. He'd only been six years old when C.J. was born.

So instead of an individual, could it be a *kind* of man she was targeting? Maybe her father left them to be a wheeler-dealer on Wall Street, and she was holding a grudge against financiers of every stripe.

"That's nonsense," he said out loud.

With just her desk lamp to light the way, he methodically went through everything on her desk, finding several orders for barn renovations and a few letters from happy customers. Cheery, but hardly relevant.

He also found quite a few things relating to the stock market, including some basic texts on how to buy and sell. But there was also a big fat tome on securities regulation, and another on mergers and acquisitions. All of that seemed a little strange. That was what *he* did.

Had she been reading up on him? *Rampant paranoia,* he told himself. But he couldn't help wondering if this was related to his rumored takeover of the fireworks factory. Could C.J. be working for Buzz, trying to confuse and distract Rowan long enough to screw up any takeover plans?

"She's not working for Buzz. She doesn't even like Buzz," he said loudly.

He moved on to the filing cabinets, but they were locked. Looking for a key, he pulled open her desk drawer, expecting to find some paperclips and a few rubber bands. But what he discovered was the other half of his bottle rocket.

It was just lying there, serene and untouched. He grabbed it and the one in his pocket in the same motion, slamming them together viciously. They fitted, all right.

The jig was up.

Cinderella was absolutely, positively, no doubt about it, Clementine Bede. He had her dead to rights.

And then the phone rang.

He jumped back, startled, his heart racing as the thing blared at him. After several rings, a message machine picked it up, and he heard C.J.'s recorded voice go through the usual routine.

When it was her turn, the caller said politely, "Hello, dear, this is Miss Pru. I saw the light go on at the office, and I wondered whether anything was wrong. It's not like you to work so late."

His first reaction was to kill the lights, but that would've been even more suspicious. Nonetheless, he ducked behind the desk, trying to figure out where the old lady was watching from. He could verify the fact that she was not at C.J.'s house, and he thought the next closest place was at least a quarter of a mile away. What could she see from a quarter of a mile away? And why was she looking?

The only thing he could figure out was that Clementine's neighbor had a telescope trained on her place. Spooky.

"Well," Miss Pru continued, "I'll speak to you some other time, my dear. Remember, you still haven't told me what happened at Mr. McKenna's house, and I'm very anxious to hear the details."

Rowan almost choked on that one. C.J. was sharing *details* with the elderly woman next door? Once Miss Pru found out about what happened in the hot tub, she was going to have a stroke!

But it did give him the idea to rewind the phone messages to see if there was anything else interesting. There was. Earlier in the day, Miss Pru had left a message about "getting the ball gown back from the cleaners in Milwaukee" and another one about finding fake fingernails in her attic.

It looked as if he'd solved the mystery of where Clementine was getting her Cinderella wardrobe. Smiling grimly he said, "So Miss Pru is playing fairy godmother. That sly dog."

He recalled very clearly their picnic discussion regarding the photo in the paper. *"You might be the only one who can identify her,"* he'd said. *"I might indeed,"* Miss Pru had responded.

Rowan shook his head. Taken in by a pretty face and an old lady. What was he reduced to?

He suddenly realized he'd better get out of there before Miss Pru called next door to the house and alerted C.J. to the fact that a burglar was ransacking her office and listening to her phone messages. With the whole bottle rocket still clasped firmly in his hand, Rowan swiftly replaced everything else he'd moved.

With the light still burning on C.J.'s desk, he slipped out the front door and hiked back to where he'd stashed his getaway car, all the while pondering his little foray into crime. Well, he couldn't call it a complete success, since he still hadn't figured out the goal of all this deception, but it wasn't a complete failure, either.

He made a fist around the little bottle rocket. He had the whole rocket back together where it belonged. And if he had his way, it wouldn't be long before he and Clementine were just as tight.

Bbbbrrrrring.

C.J. sat up in bed. The phone. Groggy and unfocused, she reached for it.

"Hello?" she asked.

"Clementine, is that you? I've been so worried!" Miss Pru's voice declared.

She sat up, focusing on the clock. One twenty-five. She couldn't have been in bed for more than a few minutes. Yet she'd already fallen half asleep. Obviously a guilty conscience was not affecting her sleeping habits any.

"Worried?" she asked Miss Pru. "Why?"

"Well, it's all the goings-on at your house, my dear. It's so very late at night for lights to be switching on and off like a Christmas tree."

"I came home late," she explained. "I went right to bed, so the lights were only on a little while. Why did that upset you?"

"But I could see lights coming from your house for some time," Miss Pru insisted. "Then they switched off, and not five minutes later, came back on. And then your office lit up! I was so surprised."

"My office?" Carrying the phone with her, C.J. shimmied out of bed and went to the window. With the shade up, she saw exactly what Miss Pru was talking about. "You're right. It looks like my desk lamp is on. I wonder why?"

"You don't suppose it's a prowler, do you?"

"Oh, I don't think so. Probably just a short in the wires or something." Yawning widely she sat down on the bed. "I'm sure it's nothing to worry about, Miss Pru. Let's just go back to sleep, shall we?"

"Well, as long as I have you, I did want to know how it went last night." The old lady's voice dropped a notch, into a more confidential register. "Was the young man happy to see you?"

"Not at first." She cleared her throat, remembering his naked body rising from the steam in that damn hot tub. Good thing Miss Pru couldn't see the warm color C.J. felt surging to her cheeks. It wouldn't take a rocket scientist to gauge that reaction.

"But later," she managed, "later, I think you could definitely say he was glad to, um, see me. We had a . . . lovely time."

The whole scene in the whirlpool came flooding back, and her face flushed hotter. *"I've seen this picture in my head for a long time,"* he'd said, as the bubbling water sluiced over her overheated skin and Rowan's gaze licked her bare breasts.

"Oh my," she gasped.

"What is it?" Miss Pru asked. "Are you all right, my dear?"

"I'm fine. I'm fine." She raised a hand to her flaming cheeks. "Just a little . . . disoriented, waking up this way."

"I am sorry. But, Clementine, I simply had to know what the next installment was. I hope you'll forgive me."

"Of course. No problem."

"And did he recognize you this time?" Miss Pru asked eagerly.

"No, he didn't." C.J. felt a sharp stab of disappointment, even though she knew that was the way she'd wanted things. What would she have done if he *had* recognized her? "Definitely better this way," she said resolutely.

"Oh, dear. I really thought *this* time . . ."

"My disguise is just too good, I guess," C.J. offered. "He's not going to see through it."

"I suppose not." There was a pause. "But you said *going to,* Clementine. That implies that this is going to continue. You're not going to risk it again, are you?"

"I—I haven't decided yet," she hedged. But she knew she had.

Lying in his arms, she'd been greedy for his love; she'd revelled in it, drunk it down like fine wine. But she still felt like a woman dying of thirst. Now that she knew what love tasted like, how could she stay away?

"If you do visit him again," Miss Pru said delicately, "perhaps the honorable course would be to arrive as the *real* you, my dear."

"But he's not in love with the real me," she said slowly. "He wants Cinderella. And if she's what he wants, then she's what he'll get."

SHE RUSHED through work, rescheduling clients and shoveling bits and pieces of her work load off onto other, less stressful days. Who could wrangle with lumberyards and stockbrokers when Rowan's arms were waiting?

Of course, his arms wouldn't be waiting until well after dark. So she sat dutifully at her desk, even though she didn't do a darn thing. Most of the time she spent staring into space and heaving moody sighs.

At the first moment she could reasonably call it a day, she shut up her office and took off across the lawn for home, planning a quick shower and then a long, painstaking change into her other persona. She took her time, covering herself with perfumes and creams, applying the whole parade of makeup, doing her hair up perfectly... She ought to have had this routine down to a science by now.

And then she stood there in her robe, frowning at the assortment of white dresses lying across her bed. Which one would she wear tonight? Good old Rainy

Day had trotted over about six of them, even though she clearly didn't understand the fascination.

"Why do they all have to be white? I mean, they're okay, but I've never seen you wear anything like any of these."

C.J. had only shrugged. "I've developed a taste for white dresses all of a sudden," she murmured. Although whatever dress she chose wouldn't stay on long.

It was brazen and shameless of her, but all day long she'd been running over the scenario she was hoping she'd be walking into. Just as before, she would arrive, and without preliminaries, he'd rip off her clothes. And then he would carry her off to bed before the door had even shut behind her.

They wouldn't waste time on small talk, they wouldn't turn on the lights and Rowan wouldn't ask even one question about who she was or why she came to him this way.

He would just make love to her.

Again and again, every way, everywhere. C.J. shivered. It was stranger and sexier than anything she'd ever imagined, and she was addicted to this dark dream.

Quickly she grabbed up a white lace T-shirt dress and slipped it on over her head, careful not to disrupt her rollers. It only took a few minutes to get her clothes on, and she was almost ready. Her hands were shaking as she brushed out her hair and gave her makeup a final touch-up.

Okay, so it was still light outside, not even eight o'clock. So she'd be early this time.

C.J. waited, completely dressed, watching the hands on the clock move with exasperating slowness, until finally, at nine o'clock, she felt it was dark enough to make her move. It had to be dark enough.

She was going now, anyway.

She parked in the same place, and hiked over the same way. His house looked just the way it had before, but this time there were no lights from the deck. This time, she went up to the front door. Behind the screen, the heavy wooden door was hanging open a few inches, as if left like that by way of invitation.

Who was he inviting? Thieves? Timber wolves? Or wandering Cinderellas?

"Rowan?" she called out softly.

And the door was wrenched open from the inside. "I wondered whether you'd come."

"I couldn't stay away," she whispered, in Cinderella's patented husky tones.

"Do you have a cold?" he asked innocently.

"Why do you ask?"

"You seem to have a frog in your throat."

What was that supposed to mean? She gave him a suspicious look, but she decided to ignore the unusual comment. "I always sound like this," she said throatily.

Behind her, she could almost swear he muttered, "No, you don't," but it wasn't quite distinct enough to catch. "Come on in," he said louder. And then he took her hand, pulling her inside the dark, shadowy house and closing the door behind her.

"It's very dark in here," she said, trying not to trip over anything.

"I thought that's the way you'd like it. Don't women of mystery prefer the dark?"

Well, actually she did. In theory. In reality, it was sort of weird and spooky. Her fantasy of a mad night of passion hadn't included details like bumping her shin on the coffee table. Didn't he know he was supposed to be whisking her off to the boudoir?

Instead he took her hand in his, raising it to his lips. But he went no further than a long, curious look at her fingers. "What happened?" he asked, raising an eyebrow.

"What happened to what?"

"Your fingernails." He nibbled the tip of each finger, one by one, taking forever, driving her crazy, as C.J. just stood there, trying to remember to breathe. "You had long fingernails before."

"I must've changed my mind. On the long or short fingernail question, I mean." She winced at how lame that sounded.

How could she have forgotten her fingernails? Anxiously she searched his face. Would this be the straw that broke the camel's back and gave her away?

But, no. He just kept watching her, giving her that same enigmatic, cool stare, as if she were a bug under a microscope. This wasn't how it was supposed to be happening at all.

He was supposed to be so hot and bothered that he didn't notice anything but the passion between them. So why was he so fascinated by meaningless details like her voice and her fingernails?

"You don't seem very happy to see me," she said reluctantly.

"Oh, I'm very happy." Still holding her hand, he drew her back a few steps, onto the couch with him. It was so dark that she didn't realize that's what it was until they hit it. He sat down first and then pulled her down, hard, into his lap.

"I'm very happy to have you here, in my hands," he murmured, slipping her hair aside and nuzzling her neck. She sighed, relaxing into his embrace. Now *this* was more like it. "You don't know how long I've been thinking about this moment," he continued, "when I can finally..."

He broke off, and his grip on her arms tightened. C.J. looked up, startled, catching what looked very much like suppressed fury flickering in his eyes. Suddenly she was afraid. But whatever it was she thought she saw, it was gone too quickly to get a good reading. His hands softened, and he began stroking her arms, kissing her neck and her jaw, easing her back into the depths of the heavy sofa.

"Is everything all right?" she asked, still a bit uneasy.

"Everything is fine," he said, in a low, seductive voice that sizzled her nerve endings. His mouth was close enough to puff hot air in her ear as he whispered, "Your skin is so soft, so smooth. I've never felt anything so luscious in my entire life. Well, maybe once..."

"Once?" She tried to sit up, but he was holding her very securely. "What do you mean?"

"Nothing, nothing," he soothed, sliding a hand up past her knee, tickling her thigh as he pulled her under him more closely.

It was very hard to think when he touched her like this, very hard to hear what he was saying. C.J. tried to hold on to some vestige of control, some shred of sense, as her body reacted with all the familiar symptoms of heat and liquid desire. He was so good at swamping her good intentions. One thumb traced the outline of her lower lip, but his other hand was getting a bit more adventurous.

"Oh," she breathed, as his fingers danced up the inside of her thigh.

"You like that, don't you?" he asked darkly.

"Yes..."

"It's so amazing," he whispered in her ear. "There are so many things about you that remind me of this other woman. Her skin is really soft and pale, too, almost exactly like yours. And her eyes go wide when I surprise her, just like yours."

"Another woman?" This time, she did sit up. "What do you mean, another woman?"

"Well," he said sensibly, leaning back on one arm, "you're hardly ever around except on the odd night you decide to waltz in and steam up my hot tub. What am I supposed to do the rest of the time?"

"What?" C.J. jumped off the couch. "Are you telling me you're fooling around?"

"Not exactly." He smiled. "But sort of."

"Oh!" She slashed a hand through her bangs, not caring if she ruined her hairdo. "I can't believe you would do this to me!"

Worse than that, she couldn't believe how casual he was about the whole thing. "Last time I was here, you told me that you loved me. What about that?" she demanded.

"The funny thing is, you've taught me something." She could see, even in the darkness, that he was no longer smiling. His jaw was clenched in a murderous line, and the expression in his eyes was cold and cynical. "You see, I've learned I can be in love with two women at the same time."

"This is impossible." She pushed away from the couch, stumbling on her way back to the door as she fought around various lumps of furniture.

But when she was almost out of his damned house, her hand on the knob, she turned back. "Who is she?"

"The other woman?"

"Yes," she said angrily. "Who is she?"

"I thought you would've guessed. She's C. J. Bede."

"C.J.... Oh, no..."

Chapter Thirteen

C.J. tossed a pile of two-by-fours onto the dusty earth, and then pulled off one of her work gloves, swiping at the dirt and perspiration on her forehead. It was hot. It was hotter than hot, with the sun blazing away up there, and the air so heavy and humid that you could almost squeeze it into a glass.

All in all, she wished she were somewhere else, somewhere cool and shady, or maybe with an air conditioner. Most of the crew was inside today, doing the interior of another barn. But this was the day she began work on Rowan's barn, and she was going to stick it out or die in the attempt.

"Can we take a break?" her young helper, a local teenager named Tripp Smalls, inquired. "I need a drink of water, Ceej."

He was the only one who called her that, and she thought it was kind of cute. As a matter of fact, Tripp was kind of cute, in a dark, brooding teenage kind of way.

Maybe she should match Tripp up with Rainy Day, who was coming along nicely as a reclamation project. As Rainy Day considered breaking into the next level of pageant, she was actually contemplating performing poetry by Walt Whitman, and she had C.J. trying to figure out how to portray "Leaves of Grass" onstage.

C.J. smiled. At least something in her life was going well.

"Go ahead, take five," she told Tripp, even though she didn't personally welcome the interruption.

If she had time to sit and think, she'd end up thinking what a mess her life was.

She hadn't seen Rowan since the night he'd told her he was two-timing her with her alter ego. Four days and four nights had passed. And she hadn't seen so much as one dark hair on that beautiful head.

She'd left a message for him yesterday, letting him know she'd found him a barn, but that was the sum total of their contact. In those four long days and four longer nights, she'd thought and thought about what it all meant. But she hadn't found any answers yet. So far, she'd run the gamut from embarrassed and confused to absolutely fire-breathing furious. At the moment, she was so mixed up that she couldn't tell a barn from a beehive.

Cinderella was retired, that was for sure. But what did she do about C.J.?

The first day, she'd clung to the silly idea that he'd meant what he said, he'd come calling, and they could progress like a normal couple. Him and C.J., that was. But he hadn't come calling.

And as C.J., she wasn't supposed to have any idea that he might have feelings for her, so she could hardly go looking for him.

Caught between a rock and a hard place, she was starting to get mad all over again. How dare he gush lovey-dovey stuff about Cinderella in C.J.'s presence, only to turn around and do the same back to Cinderella? How dared he not love either of them enough to forget about the other one?

Or maybe it had all been a convenient way to excise an unwanted woman from his life. Maybe the Prince of Takeovers had made his conquest, decided she wasn't up to snuff, and sent her packing with a trumped-up "other woman" story.

What a rat. But a very sexy rat. She might be furious with him, but she couldn't forget what it felt like to lie in his arms. She hadn't passed an hour since without remembering his lips and his hands and his strong, hard body. . . .

Now, with memories flooding her, C.J. felt the need to sit down. "I don't feel well," she murmured, and Tripp turned to her, alarmed.

"What's wrong, Ceej?"

She found a smile for him. "Just the heat. I'm going to sit in my truck and blow the AC on my face."

"You get a drink, too," Tripp ordered. "Don't want to go getting dehydrated."

"Okay, boss." She smiled, but did as she was told, stripping off her hat and her work gloves, and mopping her brow with the shirt she'd worn over her T-shirt. Crossing to the cooler, she bent and splashed water on her face, then took a paper cup back to the pickup with her.

Sure, that's all it was. The heat. With the air conditioning on full blast, C.J. lifted her ponytail and plucked at the front of her T-shirt, desperate to circulate some air. When that didn't work, she closed her eyes, rumpled her work shirt to use as a pillow and leaned back in the seat. AC or no AC, she was still light-headed, dizzy and hot enough to fry an egg on her forehead.

But then she heard the spit of tires on gravel, announcing the arrival of another vehicle.

It was Rowan's car. C.J. sat up so fast that she spilled half of the paper cup full of water down the front of her T-shirt.

His expression gave away nothing as he ambled out of the car, looking immaculate in a white shirt with the sleeves rolled up, his tie knotted loosely and a jacket tossed casually over his shoulder. He stopped near her window, and she had no choice but to roll it down to hear what he had to say.

Would this be the opening she was waiting for?

"Just came out to check on my barn," he offered coolly.

That was no opening at all. "Right over there," she said vaguely, pointing to where Tripp Smalls was sitting on a pile of lumber. "Tripp will show you what we've got."

"What about you?"

"I'm cooling off in here. I'll be with you in a minute," she mumbled.

And then she rolled up her window and locked her door, trying to get her dizzy brain to function.

What she wanted to do was drive away as fast as her trusty pickup would carry her, but that was impossible. So what was she going to do with the dad-blasted man *this* time?

Her traitorous body had an answer, as the whole thing started to tingle and hum, offering its own opinion on what to do with Rowan McKenna. But she refused to consider it.

She was just going to wait him out, hiding in the truck until he decided to go away.

"WHAT'S UP with C.J.?" he asked Tripp. He had to fight the urge not to run over there and haul her out of her truck physically. His self-control was very ragged these days, but he was still managing to hold on by a thread.

"Said she was hot."

A sudden vision of her in his hot tub hit him right between the eyes. *Hot? Was she ever.*

Rowan smiled grimly. "I like it hot," he returned with feeling.

Tripp looked over at him as if he had lost his mind. "Man, it's awful out here. And you got a tie on!"

"I know. I'm just in a good mood today."

Tripp took a long draw on the straw of his plastic water bottle. "Why are you so happy?"

Crazy as a loon was more like it. Reckless, he laughed as he said, "Maybe I'm in love."

"Oh, yeah?" Tripp glanced up with evident interest. "Anybody I know?"

That was a more interesting question than the kid realized. Rowan settled on "Maybe. Maybe not."

"Not Ceej, huh? Too bad. I thought maybe you had a thing going for her. I heard you two hung out at the picnic and the beauty pageant."

"Oh, yeah?"

Tripp shrugged. "People talk."

"Yes, they do." Rowan's lips curved in a mysterious smile. "Wish I could ease your mind. But what I feel for C.J. is very...complicated."

"Oh." Tripp gestured with his water bottle. "Well, she's sure giving you the eye from the truck." He offered a furtive grin. "I think she likes you."

"I wouldn't be a bit surprised."

"Y' know, it's funny," the boy remarked, leaning back on his two-by-fours and stretching out his dusty jeans. "At first I thought she was kind of mean, y' know, ordering me around and everything, but now I don't even mind it."

Rowan could only agree on that score as well. As C.J., she'd shown him she could be funny and smart and a very good friend. As Cinderella, she'd been wanton and reckless and amazingly uninhibited. No, he couldn't say he minded when she got bossy. In fact, he could honestly say that her pushy moments were some of her most inspired.

To Tripp, he said only, "I know what you mean."

"I never cared for any of the other Farleys," Tripp went on, slapping at his dusty pant leg. "But C.J.'s okay. My dad worked his whole life at the firecracker factory, and he says Buzz is about as big a bucket of scum as they come. But not C.J."

Rowan turned, not quite sure if he was hearing what he thought he was hearing. He felt the pulse begin to pound in his temple. "Not C.J. what?"

"She just ain't like the other Farleys."

"I don't understand."

Tripp shrugged. "Blood bein' thicker 'n water and all that. Good thing for C.J. it ain't true."

The air around him started to hum. "You're saying that the Farleys are related to C.J.? How?"

"Buzz is her daddy."

"Buzz Farley is C.J.'s father?" he shouted.

Tripp sat up quickly. "Well, not her real, you know, legal father, on account of how he married Mim Farley instead. Legalwise, I guess C.J. doesn't have one. Gee, I'm sorry, Mr. McKenna. I thought you knew. Everybody in town knows. Except for Mim and the girls. I mean, they must know, but they'd sure never admit it."

"Buzz Farley is C.J.'s father."

And suddenly it had all become clear—the sampler on her wall, the books about the stock market, the financial problems at Farley Fireworks that made it look like something funny was going on....

The hum around him accelerated to a roar.

C.J. Bede hated the man who was her father, who'd left her mother to raise her alone. Her father was Buzz Farley. C.J. hated Buzz...

Rowan shook his head, but it didn't clear his mind. All those little details were just hopping and bouncing along in there.

So C.J. was trying to take down Buzz Farley, and Farley Fireworks along with him. But then the Prince of Takeovers had come to town, and with him came the rumors, and Farley stock had started to rise.

And that's when Cinderella had appeared.

There was a certain amount of convoluted, bizarre logic to it, he supposed. If he were out of his everloving mind.

"She wanted me out of the way, safely chasing dream girls, with no time to spare for the fireworks factory." He ran a rough hand through his hair. Damn. It all added up. "She was going after Buzz and I just happened to get caught in the cross fire."

"Huh?"

"Look, Tripp," Rowan began, going for his wallet. "I need you to take the rest of the day off."

"But C.J.—"

He handed him over fifty bucks, biting out his words very tersely. "It's my barn, and I want you to take the day off."

Shrugging, Tripp backed off. After a few confused moments, he seemed happy to oblige, and he headed for a rusty Jeep parked out by the end of the road.

As he watched the kid leave, Rowan also cast a wary eye over at C.J., who was surveying the scene with increasing interest. She dangled half-in and half-out of the cab of her truck for a while, and then jumped down, with a look of grim determination on her pretty little face.

She was headed right for him, and he knew why. She was just itching to know why her employee had been dismissed without anybody asking for her approval.

Rowan was prepared for a confrontation, all right. But not exactly the one she had in mind.

As she marched toward him in her tight, worn blue jeans and the skinny white T-shirt that revealed more than it concealed, his mouth went dry. His body reacted instinctively, the way it always did when she was around, tightening into instant, rigid arousal.

Over the past few days, this little problem had been getting worse and worse. He had only himself to blame, of course, since she'd been kind enough to come right up to his front door and offer herself up like a sacrifice. Maybe if he'd pulled her inside and made love to her for a few hours, the way his body was begging him to, he wouldn't be in such dire straits now.

But he doubted it. He wasn't sure this desperate need would ever stop.

He'd been bound and determined to play a few games of his own that night, to turn her life upside down the way she'd done to his. Smarting, full of pride, ready to turn her over his knee, he'd chased her away instead.

And for the past four days, he'd let her stew. What better revenge than to tell her he was in love with her, and then hang her out to dry? It was a good thing she'd called him about the barn, though. He wasn't sure he could've been responsible for his actions if she's waited one second longer to get in touch with him.

He was still plenty angry, and plenty turned on. But at the moment, that was her problem, not his.

Right now, he was just mad enough to take what he wanted. Before he throttled her for deceiving him, for shutting him out, and worst of all, making an ass of him, he was going to get a little satisfaction for this agonizing need.

He threw his jacket down on the pile of two-by-fours and prepared to face her. "Get ready, Clementine," he said under his breath. "You and I have some pressing business to attend to."

Two or three paces away, she demanded, "Where did Tripp go?"

"I sent him away."

"Away where?"

"Away," he growled. He'd shown about as much patience as he had left, and he hauled her into his arms without further ado, knocking her damn baseball cap off with one flick of his hand.

"Rowan!" she cried, her eyes wide. "What's gotten into you?"

"You," he said roughly. He pulled her closer, one hand behind her neck, and he kissed her, hard. "I've been wanting to do this for a long time."

He cut her off before she got any further, angling his mouth to delve deeper, grinding his hips against her, demanding that she respond with all the fire and the passion she hid inside. After one night of passion and four days of hell, he was fully prepared to do his best to trip all her switches, until she whimpered and moaned for more.

He'd played the game by her rules so long that he'd almost forgotten he didn't have to. With his mouth and his tongue and his lips crushing her, conquering her, he told her now.

I can have you any time I want you, and we both know it.

"Rowan," she cried. Her knees shook as she tried to push away. "I don't think I . . ."

But it was a feeble protest. Even as her mouth formed the words, her arms slid around his waist, urging him closer.

The air around them was steamy and humid, and she was hot to the touch, damp with perspiration. Her small, soft breasts pressed against his chest through the thin fabric of her T-shirt, brushing him, teasing him. He wanted to hold her immobile, to stop the gentle motion that was driving him higher and harder than he wanted to go.

But she wouldn't stand still. Her mouth was hungry and wet under his; she was nipping at his lip, crawling up into him, acting reckless and wild.

About three more seconds of that nubile little body rubbing up against him, and he wouldn't have been able to stop. He was so turned on that he was ready to explode into a million pieces, but he still knew better than to make love out in the open on a pile of lumber.

With a muttered oath, he pushed her away from him, and then caught her wrist, towing her along in his wake as he made for cover. It wasn't pretty, just an old, abandoned barn with a tarp laid down instead of a floor, but he didn't give a damn.

"Here?" she asked.

"Here."

And then he yanked her back up against him, where she belonged. He saw shock and desire strike sparks in her golden hazel eyes as the full extent of his arousal became only too apparent, but she didn't move away. He was trying to make her mad, make her react, call him names, tell him no. But she didn't.

Instead she slid her arms around his neck, lifting her face for his kiss. But he deliberately didn't kiss her, just gazed long and hard into her eyes, daring her to look away. Her nostrils flared slightly, her lips fell open and her breasts rose and fell with her shaky breaths. But she didn't look away.

With excruciating slowness, he moved his hands over her body, claiming her as his own. His hands measured her round, firm buttocks, clasped her, pushing her into his heavy hardness, pressing her up against that greedy ache.

Her mouth fell open, and her head tipped back. She was trying not to moan, but her breath was coming in hot little pants that unwound him from the inside out.

With one hand holding her fast at the hip, the other slid up underneath her shirt, cupping her breast, squeezing, fingering the taut rosy nipple as it peaked into his palm.

Her moans grew louder, and she swayed against him, frantically trying to rub closer. Every motion begged him to touch her, stroke her, bring her relief.

But Rowan held back, fighting his own needs, his own desire. He wasn't touching anything he hadn't touched before, or seeing or hearing anything he hadn't already witnessed that night on his deck. But it was different now, in the full light of day. It was different when she was only herself, not hiding behind some disguise of dainty perfume and lace.

This time, it was real. This time, the scent of Clementine, of clean hair and honest sweat and musky woman, filled his nostrils. He loved it.

"Mmm, you smell good," he whispered, and she gave him a look of utter disbelief.

He grabbed for her T-shirt, slashing it off over her head, tearing the fragile cotton in two, and she responded in kind, ripping his shirt down the front, scattering buttons every which way and almost choking him with his tie.

They fell down onto the tarpaulin together, spinning and rolling as they carelessly discarded their shoes and their clothes and reached for each other. His pants were still around his ankles when she tangled her legs around his hips, urging him into her, and he kicked them away before he plunged heavily, deeply inside. He filled her, exposed her, drove himself hard and fierce and fast.

His voice was raw and raspy when he said, "Clementine," but he said it again and again, using her name to set the rhythm of his harsh thrusts. No mercy.

"Clementine," he repeated, making it crystal clear exactly who he was making love to.

No dreams, no fantasies. Just Clementine.

Her eyes were closed, her face glazed with pleasure, as he sank into her, pushing her harder and faster. He wanted to drink in every moment of her exquisite surrender, feel every tiny shudder of passion, hear each small moan of bliss, as he brought her over the top.

But when he felt the ripples of her body convulsing around him, he was the one who lost control.

"Clementine!" he shouted, rocketing into her, exploding in a shower of fire and sparks.

He felt like falling dead on top of her, panting and gasping, until he regained some stamina. But he pulled away, far enough to rest his hand on her cheek, to reach out tenderly and brush a sweat-slick tendril of hair away from her cheek.

It was the haunting, haunted look in her eyes that stopped him.

"Rowan," she whispered. "You know, don't you?"

A long pause hung between them.

She already knew, but he told her, anyway. "Yes, I do."

Her whole body suffused with rosy color, and she rolled away. "How long?"

He reached for his pants. Without a word, he pulled out the bottle rocket, all neatly together in one piece, and dropped it in her lap.

C.J. pressed her eyes closed. "My half disappeared the night of the Miss Firecracker pageant. Is that it? Is that when you found out?"

"Yes."

"You broke into my office, and you found the firecracker, and that was how you knew?"

"No. I knew the first moment I saw you." His voice was husky when he said, "After that night in the whirlpool, I just knew. There you were, in your jeans and a work shirt, holding a pig and talking to Rainy Day, and it hit me like a ton of bricks." His eyes narrowed. "Did you really think I could make love to you, and not notice who you were?"

Her blush intensified, and she blinked suddenly. Turning her face away, she grabbed for the closest piece of clothing—his shirt—and shrugged into it quickly. She was doing a very good impression of being humiliated and embarrassed. That was not the reaction he'd expected. His hand framed her cheek as he tugged her back around, forcing her to look at him.

"I love you, C.J. I told you that a long time ago. There's no reason to be ashamed."

"But you didn't love me. You *don't* love me!" With one fist closed around the tiny bottle rocket, she sat up and hugged her knees to her chest. "You loved *her* first."

"But she's you."

"No, she's not."

He felt like laughing, but it was too frustrating. "Then who the hell is she?"

"I don't know." She said wildly, "She's just somebody I made up. Somebody who could be all the things I'm not."

"C.J., she's all the things you are, too. For good or bad, she's you."

There was a long pause, and he could see she was trying to come to the point. "If you knew, why did you wait so long to spring it on me?"

"Mostly because I was mad, and I wanted to make you sweat. But partly because I didn't know why."

"Why what?"

"Why you did it." A bit of the old anger, the anger he thought he'd already burned off, trickled back. "I couldn't imagine any reason an otherwise sane woman would get all dressed up and try to make a fool out of me."

"I didn't want... I couldn't let..." But her explanations trailed away. "I guess things got a little out of hand."

"If that's your way of referring to dancing into my house at midnight and playing love slave," he shot back, "I'd say things got a *lot* out of hand."

That got her attention. Sitting up straighter, she looked down her nose at him with all the feisty disapproval he knew so well. "I was hardly your love slave. And don't pretend you didn't like it."

He couldn't keep the hot desire out of his gaze. He'd just had her and he already wanted her again. And he was in no position to hide it. "Oh, I liked it," he murmured, trailing a finger up and down her bare, slender leg. "I liked it just fine."

Her cheeks were pink when she said stiffly, "So did I."

A lazy smile curved his lips. "I noticed."

He let that one hang in the air. Let her deal with it. It was her fault.

After a moment, she apparently decided that the best tactic was simply to ignore the obvious.

"So why didn't you tell me you knew?" she demanded. "We could've had this out days ago. Instead, I've been miserable. I hated deceiving you. I hated losing my half of the bottle rocket—I couldn't figure out where it had run off to. But most of all, I hated falling in love with you, not sure which one of us you wanted or what the hell was going on. You know, I've really come to hate her and her stupid white dresses."

"I like you any way you come, C.J. White dresses. Blue jeans." He whispered, "Or nothing at all."

She trembled, reaching out to touch his cheek. "So why now?"

"I couldn't wait another second." He spoke softly, watching her steadily. "And Tripp let something slip today, something the whole town apparently knows, but nobody was willing to tell me. When I heard it, everything fell into place."

"Oh, no." Her voice was barely a whisper. "Not about Buzz. You don't know about Buzz."

"I know he's your father. I guessed the rest."

She swallowed. "What rest?"

"Quit playing cute with me, Clementine." He was starting to work up some steam, and he pulled on his pants, unwilling to have an argument while he was at a distinct disadvantage in the clothing department. "The jig is up. I know it all. But you're still refusing to come clean with me."

She sat there, stubbornly silent, and he sighed, jamming his hands in his pockets. "I know Buzz is your father. I know you're trying to get back at him for what he did to your mother. So far, so good?"

She bit her lip.

He continued, "I figure you've been manipulating Farley Fireworks stock somehow or other. Before people got wind of a possible takeover, their stock was taking a nosedive. That was one very suspicious nosedive. I don't know exactly what you did, but I'd be willing to wager it wasn't entirely legal."

She raised her chin. "I don't know what you mean."

"Oh, yes, you do," he returned severely. "What did you try? Phone calls, here and there, like a few orders canceled or rerouted? Some insider tips planted with stockbrokers that the plant had union troubles, or was losing business? That kind of stuff is securities fraud, honeybun."

"You can't prove anything."

"I don't need to." He paced off a path in front of her. "That's easy enough for a smart girl like you. But the tricky part is where I come in." C.J. started to speak, but Rowan was on a roll, and he raised a hand to forestall her. "I've got the basic idea. Either you decided I needed to be sidetracked from taking over Farley Fireworks, and you thought a little romance would do the trick, or else you were afraid I'd go for one of the Farley girls and bail the factory out on her behalf." He gave her a look of definite disgust. "That really hurts, Clementine. If you thought for one second I would ever, *ever,* look at either of those twits—"

"I didn't," she whispered.

"Well, good," he said darkly. "I may be a fool, but I'm not that big a fool."

"No, never," she assured him.

"Damn right. So this was all just to sidetrack me, huh? This elaborate hocus-pocus was all just to keep me away from Farley Fireworks?"

"I don't even know anymore," she said miserably. "I mean, I know I had good reasons when I started, but things ran away with me so quickly that I just couldn't stop!"

"Is that the best you can do?"

She hitched up her knees and laid her head on them, giving in completely. "I wanted to know what you were doing in town, and I thought you were a lot more likely to spill your guts to a beautiful, sexy siren than to plain old me. And then I couldn't stop. I really liked you, and you really liked me! But you didn't recognize me."

"Sorry."

"Oh, it's okay." She shrugged. "I kind of got used to the idea that I was invisible as long as I wore my jeans and my baseball cap."

He knelt down beside her then, taking her into his arms one more time. "Not to me, Clementine. Never to me."

"I can't believe this is happening." She snuggled closer, sliding her arms around his bare chest. "I thought you would hate me if you ever found out."

"I considered it."

She dropped a small kiss on his collar bone, and another under his ear. "Especially the part about

Buzz. Who would ever want to sleep with someone from his gene pool?''

"Let's leave him and his genes out of this," Rowan said gruffly.

Her hazel eyes held him, as she asked quietly, "Are you really sure you love both parts of me, both C.J. and Cinderella?"

"Yes." He was gratified to see relief and love and honesty shining from her eyes. "I can't tell you how wonderful it is to know I'm not losing my mind, that I'm not in love with two women at the same time, and to put together both halves of the woman I love."

"Thank you," she said, squeezing him in a ferocious grip.

"There's just one thing..."

She glanced up, apprehensive. "What?"

"Your revenge plot. The illegal stuff has to go, so we're going to have to work on restructuring a few things. I would suggest we work on taking the factory away from Buzz, rather than running the place into the ground...."

Frowning, she murmured, "I don't think I'm going to like this."

Rowan gave her the full benefit of his most dazzling smile. He slipped one hand up under the edge of his shirt, the one she looked so fetching in, sketching a path up the smooth contour of her thigh. "Trust me."

C.J. caught his hand, but she made no move to take it away. As a matter of fact, she inched it higher. With a very inviting smile of her own, she whispered, "I think that can be arranged."

Chapter Fourteen

"What a lovely day for a tea party," Miss Pru said happily. She lifted the lovely silver teapot and inquired, "Need a touch more, Ivy, dear? Rowan? Clementine?"

"No, thank you," they all hastened to tell her. Sitting under a sweeping sugar maple on Miss Pru's lawn, they had all stuffed themselves with scones and tiny cakes and dainty finger sandwiches, and they were positively floating in tea.

C.J. smiled at Rowan, who was looking very dishy in a cream-colored Gatsby suit they'd found in Miss Pru's attic. It was quite a shock to find that he liked playing dress-up almost as much as she did. Of course, he also liked playing un-dress-up, and unwrapping her from all those fur coats and boas and pantaloons and corsets. Luckily Miss Pru seemed to have figured out that they enjoyed private costume parties, and she had given them free rein with her attic.

But today's little fete, complete with lace tablecloths and fine china, with all of them decked out in the finest the Roaring Twenties had to offer, was a group celebration. This group of co-conspirators was getting very near its goal, and they were enjoying themselves. Even her mother, a person she would never have imagined getting into the spirit of things, was beaming. She was also looking extremely pretty in a big picture hat and a pale yellow silk dress from Miss Pru's collection.

"To you," Rowan proposed, lifting his teacup and offering C.J. a mysterious, seductive smile. She knew what that smile meant, and she wondered how long he was going to behave himself at the tea party before he pulled her away and started a celebration of his own.

"To Clementine," her mother and her fairy godmother joined in.

But C.J. had a toast of her own. Carelessly tossing her napkin across the lap of her ivory lace dress, C.J. raised her tea cup. "To the best bunch of accomplices in the entire world."

"Hear, hear!" Miss Pru added. "Oh, that reminds me. Did I tell you that my stockbroker found another fifty shares? A very nice lady in Milwaukee seems to have been sitting on them, but she's willing to sell. He called me just this morning."

"But that's great." C.J. almost knocked her napkin into the jam pot in her excitement. "We're so close even I don't believe it."

"We're at the threshold," Rowan declared. "And before Buzz Farley knows what hit him, we'll be kicking in the door."

"To fifty-one percent of Farley Fireworks!" C.J. began, and they all raised their teacups in approval. Under the table, she could feel Rowan's free hand tickling her knee. She brushed him away, but his fingers came right back.

"Oh, my, my!" Miss Pru said suddenly, standing up from the table. "It seems to me this occasion calls for more than mere tea. I think I have a bottle of sherry inside. Would you care to help me, Ivy? We can bring out some glasses and have a real toast."

"Oh, I don't need any sherry," Ivy said innocently.

"Yes, yes," Miss Pru insisted. "We all need sherry."

Much to Clementine's surprise, Rowan put in, "I think it's a wonderful idea."

Ivy seemed confused, but Miss Pru took her by the elbow and guided her along back to the house, whispering meaningfully all the way.

"You don't like sherry," C.J. said coyly.

He grinned. "I know."

"So why did you send those poor little ladies all the way up to the house for something you don't want?"

"Because," he whispered, edging her around so that they were practically in the same chair, "I wanted to be alone with you."

Her lips curved into a lazy smile. "Oh, I see."

"Out here in the sunshine on such a beautiful day," he said lightly, tipping up her chin with one finger, "with such a beautiful lady at my side, with that beautiful lady's goal so close at hand, it seemed the perfect time."

He lowered his lips to hers, lingering in the sweetest of kisses, and as always, Rowan took her breath away. C.J. tangled her arms around his neck. "The perfect time to kiss me?" she murmured.

"The perfect time to ask you to marry me."

"What?" As she watched in amazement, he pushed his chair away and got down on one knee in the grass. "Come on, Rowan," she said with a laugh, "you're going to get grass stains on the knees of your white suit."

He sent her a sideways glance. "Better than getting grass stains on the back of your white dress if I do what I'd really like to do."

"Rowan—" she protested, but he was having none of it.

With her hand in his, he gave her the full benefit of his gorgeous gaze, and then he asked, in a husky sort of voice, "Miss Clementine Jemima Bede, would you do me the honor of becoming my wife?"

She didn't know what she planned to say, but it would only come out one way. "Yes," she whispered. He picked her up off the chair and hugged her tight.

"Thank God."

"What's all this?" Ivy asked, as she and Miss Pru came back with the sherry.

C.J. was still firmly attached to Rowan's shirt-front, but she heard him say, "Ladies, it looks like we have something new to celebrate."

"Who is it?" Mím demanded, tugging on her husband's sleeve. "The new guy should be here in five minutes, and everyone wants to know who it is, and you refuse to tell me. It's not bad enough that you couldn't hold on to the business. No! Now you have to make me look even more foolish by not knowing who's bought out my own factory!"

"It's my damn factory, not yours!" Buzz yelled back. "I told you before and I'll tell you again, I don't know who the new owner is. All the info I got was that it was some outfit called the Hellhath Holding Company, and I told you that already. Now what kinda name is Hellhath, I'd like to know?"

Mim pursed her lips together and stalked off to talk it over with her cronies. The new owner was arriving in a moment, and she, Mim Farley, did not know who this interloper, this viper in the bosom of Sparks, would turn out to be. It was galling.

Half the town was lined up outside the beleaguered factory, eager to catch a glimpse of the person who would now be Sparks's biggest man, by virtue of owning its biggest business.

Most people still had their money bet on Rowan McKenna, but a few thought he was too obvious to be the secret buyer. But if not him, who?

Two long black limousines pulled slowly down the circular driveway in front of the factory, one right after the other, and the crowd began to stir. "Two limousines? Why two? Who is it? Can you see? Who do you think it is?" they all buzzed.

The first limo pulled to a stop, and a liveried driver stepped smartly around to open the swanky, backward door. And out stepped . . .

Rowan McKenna.

"It *is* him!" Bitty Delmar cried out, doing her civic duty to inform those who were farther back in the crowd, without as good as view as hers.

But then Rowan offered his hand to someone in the limo, and another person was guided out onto the sidewalk.

"C. J. Bede!" the call went back, echoing as it reached all the layers of people lined up for a look.

And then Rowan moved to the door of the second limo, helping a third person and then a fourth person out of the car.

"Ivy Bede!" they all shouted. "And Miss Prudence Hopmiller!"

The four VIPs, all dressed nattily in dark suits and dresses, made their way through the crowd. It was rather disappointing, several people remarked, that it had turned out to be Rowan McKenna, after all, and he'd simply brought some friends along to watch as he signed the papers.

But as they neared the front door of the Firecracker Factory, Rowan and his party paused. They seemed to be conferring with Buzz, whispering something back and forth, as Buzz's face got redder and redder and the whispering got louder and louder.

"I won't do it!" he bellowed. And then he stomped off inside the factory.

"Ahem." It was C. J. Bede, clearing her throat, raising her hand in the air. "If I could have your attention, please?"

What was this all about? The crowd grumbled and mumbled and milled around for a better look.

"Excuse me, everyone. I know you're all very anxious to know what's going to happen at the factory, so we decided we ought to make some kind of public statement before we do the formal turning over of the keys and such. Unfortunately Buzz has been called away unexpectedly, so I will make the announcement myself."

"Why is she talking?" Geneva Lugden asked Mim. "If he bought the factory, why is she talking?"

C.J. gave them all a bright smile. "So the first thing I would like to tell you is that the Hellhath Holding Company, of which I am the president, has just purchased a majority interest in Farley Fireworks."

"*She* bought it?" Mim shrieked. "It can't be!"

"Well, Mim, it is," C.J. said cheerfully. "However, one of our vice-presidents, my mother, Miss Ivy Bede, will be assuming control of this particular company."

"Ivy Bede?" Mim's face took on a rather violent shade of purple as she pushed her way up to the front of the pack. Right in front of C.J., she roared, "Ivy Bede is running *my* company?"

"Why, Mim, I think you've got it." And C.J. made a grand display of handing some official looking documents over to her mother. "Since Buzz Farley acted in the lowest and most despicable way possible to my mother some thirty years ago—"

Her words were interrupted by a renewed uproar in the crowd, as the people up on old Sparks gossip informed those around them exactly what Buzz had done to Ivy thirty years ago.

"Since Buzz Farley acted in such a despicable manner," C.J. repeated, enjoying that part of her little speech, "it seems only fitting that my mother will now be his new boss. When she has made a firm decision on whether Buzz will still be an employee of the fireworks factory, I'm sure she'll let you know."

Bending close to her mother, she gave her a quick hug and whispered, "You're going to be great, Mom."

"Don't worry about a thing," Ivy said, with a renewed sense of purpose. "I'm really going to enjoy having Buzz Farley report to me."

"Atta girl!" Rowan told her, giving his almost-mother-in-law a kiss on the cheek. And then he took C.J.'s hand firmly in his and began to thread his way back through the crowd to their limo.

"Where are they going?" Mim demanded, and the people around her took up the call. "Yeah, where are they going?"

Rowan and C.J. stopped near the limo, but it was Miss Pru who spoke. "Silence!" she commanded, in her most patrician voice, and the entire crowd fell completely quiet. "Ivy and I have some papers to sign here at the factory," she continued, "and a meeting to convene with the very rude and unpleasant Mr. Farley."

"But where are *they* going?" Mim asked again.

"Clementine and her young man are going to be married today, as it happens, at my house. Now they've decided that they'd like a private ceremony, with only a few friends present. So as soon as we get our duties here out of the way, we're going to join them to witness their wedding." Miss Pru smiled. "I'm the best man."

"He's really going to marry her? Well, I never," one of Mim's friends sniffed.

"In the spirit of camaraderie and goodwill, I am inviting all of you—" Miss Pru looked down her nose at Mim "—even the Farleys, to join us later this evening for a postwedding soiree at my home."

"A party!" the crowd took up the cry. "A party, everyone."

Rowan save Miss Pru a jaunty salute. "Don't be long!" he called out.

Miss Pru and Ivy stood there, arm in arm, waving them away. Together they shouted, "You can't get married without us!"

As THE DRIVER pulled them away from the firecracker factory, Rowan popped the cork on the champagne and poured a glass for his favorite business tycoon. "You got what you wanted. Buzz is furious, Mim's having fits and your mother is sweetly avenged. How does it feel?"

"Not as good as I thought it would," she admitted. She leaned back into the luxurious cushions of the limousine, stretching her legs out over Rowan's expensive trousers. "Revenge *is* sweet, but I discovered something a lot more important about myself."

Rowan pulled her over into his lap, sipping from her champagne flute and nuzzling her neck. "And what's that, my love?"

C.J. smiled dreamily. "That I can love someone. That someone can love me, for who I am. That I can be happy, every day, because I'm so lucky."

"Cheers," he offered, clinking his glass against her. "I love you, Clementine. Now can we finally get married?"

She glanced at her watch. "If everything goes as planned, it should all be over in about three hours. That's if mother and Miss Pru get there, and if the minister doesn't get lost...."

"Driver," Rowan called out. "Step on it. We've got a wedding to make."

And so Clementine Jemima Bede relaxed into the embrace of her charming Prince of Takeovers.

And they all lived happily ever after....

When the only time you have for yourself is...

STOLEN *moments* ™

Christmas is such a busy time—with shopping, decorating, writing
cards, trimming trees, wrapping gifts....

When you do have a few *stolen moments* to call your own, treat yourself
to a brand-new *short* novel. Relax with one of our Stocking Stuffers—
or with all six!

Each STOLEN MOMENTS title
is a complete and original contemporary romance that's the perfect
length for the busy woman of the nineties! Especially at Christmas...

And they make perfect **stocking stuffers,** too! (For your mother,
grandmother, daughters, friends, co-workers, neighbors, aunts,
cousins—all the other women in your life!)

Look for the STOLEN MOMENTS display in December

STOCKING STUFFERS:

HIS MISTRESS Carrie Alexander
DANIEL'S DECEPTION Marie DeWitt
SNOW ANGEL Isolde Evans
THE FAMILY MAN Danielle Kelly
THE LONE WOLF Ellen Rogers
MONTANA CHRISTMAS Lynn Russell

HSM2

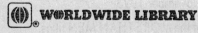

HARLEQUIN®

AMERICAN ◆ ROMANCE®

Have Yourself an American Romance Christmas!

Christmas is the one time of year when dreams—no matter how small or how large—come true with a wish . . . and a kiss. In December, we're celebrating this spirit—and bringing our dashing heroes right under the mistletoe, just for you!

'Tis the season...

#513
FALLING ANGEL
by Anne Stuart

#514
YES, VIRGINIA . . .
by Peg Sutherland

#515
**NO ROOM AT
THE INN**
by Linda Randall Wisdom

#516
**MERRY CHRISTMAS,
BABY**
by Pamela Browning

SEASON

Relive the romance...
Harlequin and Silhouette
are proud to present

A program of collections of three complete novels by the most-requested
authors with the most-requested themes. Be sure to look for one volume each
month with three complete novels by top-name authors.

In September: **BAD BOYS**   Dixie Browning
                                     Ann Major
                                     Ginna Gray
No heart is safe when these hot-blooded hunks are in town!

In October: **DREAMSCAPE**   Jayne Ann Krentz
                                     Anne Stuart
                                     Bobby Hutchinson
Something's happening! But is it love or magic?

In December: **SOLUTION: MARRIAGE** Debbie Macomber
                                       Annette Broadrick
                                       Heather Graham Pozzessere
Marriages in name only have a way of leading to love....

Available at your favorite retail outlet.

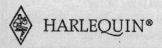
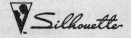

1993 Keepsake

CHRISTMAS

Stories

Capture the spirit and romance of Christmas with KEEPSAKE CHRISTMAS STORIES, a collection of three stories by favorite historical authors. The perfect Christmas gift!

Don't miss these heartwarming stories, available in November wherever Harlequin books are sold:

ONCE UPON A CHRISTMAS by Curtiss Ann Matlock
A FAIRYTALE SEASON by Marianne Willman
TIDINGS OF JOY by Victoria Pade

ADD A TOUCH OF ROMANCE TO YOUR HOLIDAY SEASON WITH KEEPSAKE CHRISTMAS STORIES!

HX93

**Fifty red-blooded, white-hot, true-blue hunks
from every State in the Union!**

Look for MEN MADE IN AMERICA! Written by some
of our most poplar authors, these stories feature fifty of
the strongest, sexiest men, each from a different state in
the union!

Two titles available every other month at your favorite
retail outlet.

In November, look for:

STRAIGHT FROM THE HEART by Barbara Delinsky
(Connecticut)
AUTHOR'S CHOICE by Elizabeth August (Delaware)

In January, look for:

DREAM COME TRUE by Ann Major (Florida)
WAY OF THE WILLOW by Linda Shaw (Georgia)

You won't be able to resist MEN MADE IN AMERICA!
